"Tremendous. Haack has managed to make love not war. In honoring WWII Czech Air Force and Royal Air Force pilot Václav Hájek's unsung life, she leaves us with a glimmer of resounding hope that it really will all work out in the ultimate end. What we do here now matters for Eternity."

"Dive in. Trust the process. Enjoy any kaleidoscopic inconsistency. It ties together beautifully in the end."

"Mythical and mystical, this is an intimate memoir of humbly-cloaked glory, honor, and immortality. Think Marcus Aurelius' <u>Meditations</u> meets Téa Obreht's <u>The Tiger's Wife</u>, and add a poignant twist of intention to persist in doing good, doing right. Haack speaks to our patient waiting hearts and reminds us to remember."

# PETAL

## AND

# POULTICE

~

*Memories of*

*Destiny*

**Anne Květa Haack**

There once was a flower
Who climbed up a tower.
The wind blew her off
But then had to cough
And gave her back her power.

"Flower Power"
c. 1983, by Anne Květa Haack

# Prologue: Ladybugs and Blossoms

*T*here once was a wine curiously called Predator that bore a ladybug on its seal. For a time, I loved that particular Zinfandel and made it the house wine frankly because it drank like a meal. Names carry stories, and I soon learned that ladybugs can function in a protective capacity as predators feeding on insects that would otherwise cause harm to the old vines on which those grapes grow. For this reason, I came not only to think of ladybugs as splashy and cute but also to admire and respect them as worthy of an emblem.

Welcoming one of these tiny travelers, making a whimsical wish, then blowing it on its merry way took on a deeper resonance in tune with a divinely well-woven world. Prompting nostalgic glimmers of hope in the hearts of lovers and little girls, inflicting death upon harmful critters, and effecting wines it will never taste, this tiny beetle gives a glimpse to joy and sorrow and purpose. "Nothing can seem extraordinary until you have discovered what is ordinary," C.S. Lewis acknowledges. Our roles in life come together in a manner that all too often looks and feels like the knotty stringy underbelly of a needlepoint. Fathoming this embroidered canvas from above through the soulful sweetness of Heavenly grace moves the mundane into the majestic.

First-named Anne with an "e" after the fictional Anne of Green Gables, I was middle-named Květa after the very real Květa Anna Marie Hájek (née Mach), my mother Olga's mother. In Prague back when Prague was part of Czechoslovakia, Květa met and married the man who would become my maternal grandpa, Václav Hájek, affectionately known as Vendí. Květa means blossom, or flower, and if one goes to Prague in the Czech Republic today and finds a květiny, one can buy flowers there. All blossoms are flowers, though not all flowers are blossoms. Quite literally, blossoms provide pollen to pollinators such as bees, and bees are then able to share that pollen with trees so that trees can bear fruit. Still more marvelously, even a fruit tree blossom's wind-blown petals can provide poultices if not panaceas.

The created universe has a harmonic. Were the world a perfect art, with delight and purpose we would each recognize our integral part. That we could each act constructively, cheerfully, and bravely so as to effect this restoration of paradise humbles and ennobles. It hearkens of shalom.

Ours is of course a broken world. As a Connecticut schoolgirl on a seventh-grade French class field trip to Québec, I noticed the Canadian province's official motto gracing its license plates: *Je me souviens*. It indicates a requisite remembrance of past so as to inform the future and better intuit our unique and collective roles now. Looking back helps us go forward.

Time does have its way of seeming to fold in on itself. Past, present, and future can blend kaleidoscopically with marvelous dimension. It feels strangely beautiful to perceive even fleetingly how significantly particular our life paths and placements can be in the restoration of a harmonious world. In these moments and modalities, volition flows into destiny while the past pours into the present.

What if the history of the world is really one giant love story, echoing from the cosmic to the subatomic with the interpersonal in between? God is a great author. Like ladybugs, we might never know much of what we help restitute. This is a story about how paying it forward pays the past and repairs us to the present. Most of it is very much true, and the rest is heuristic if not very much true in an alternate universe. Let it seep into your soul.

# Love is Swell and War is Hell

*O*n Thursday, 30 January 1913, when World
War I had yet to begin, a no-confidence motion
passed in the Reichstag regarding the German
Empire's Chancellor, the Ottoman Empire refused
to surrender its Aegean Islands to the Great Powers
as the First Balkan War came to a close, and my
grandpa Václav Hájek was born in Prague.
Ultimately commissioned to the rank of Squadron
Leader flying Spitfires with the Royal Air Force
(RAF) decades hence, he helped save the day in the
Battle of Britain, became a Major on the General
Staff, emigrated to the United States of America at
the age of 42, and lived to be 86.

On Saturday, 30 August 1924, the moon passed
between the earth and the sun, and Květa Anna
Marie Mach was born in the Bohemian village of
Ohnišov. She married this man Václav Hájek in
Czechoslovakia 22 years hence. On Saturday, 3
January 1948, Václav and Květa in Prague
welcomed into the world a baby girl named Olga
who would eventually become my mother. That
very same day of Olga's birth, British Prime
Minister Clement Attlee noted that "today in
Eastern Europe the Communist Party, while
overthrowing the economic tyranny of landlordism
and capitalism, has renounced the doctrines of
individual freedom and political democracy and

rejected the whole spiritual heritage of Western Europe." Eighteen months later, Václav and Květa left Czechoslovakia forever. They brought baby Olga with them into exile.

What had happened was this: When Czechoslovakia fell to Germany in 1939 most of the Czech pilots left and soon flew for France. Václav flew for France in North Africa. After the defeat of France in 1940, Václav fled through Casablanca to England and joined the RAF. In England, the experienced Czech fighter pilots comprised three RAF squadrons that fought in the Battle of Britain and the rest of World War II. Václav flew Spitfires and with his 313th Fighter Squadron shot down German planes on various missions.

After World War II ended in 1945, Václav and the heroic Czech pilots returned home to Czechoslovakia. Václav Hájek met Květa Mach at the University of Prague. Meanwhile, the Communists who had liberated Prague were resisting all post-war efforts by these Czech pilots to resurrect the Czech Air Force. When the Communists imprisoned Václav's superior officer in 1948, shortly after baby Olga's arrival, Václav and Květa quietly decided to escape their homeland, and they agreed to bring their baby girl.

The three of them paid one final visit to Ohnišov, a village 160 kilometers from Prague with a population of 500, and spent time on the farm where Květa's family had lived since they founded the settlement in 1753. Telling anyone in the family what they were planning could have endangered the family, so they told no one. 1948 is the last time that Květa's father Václav Mach would ever see his daughter, his son-in-law, and his granddaughter. He would never forget them; moreover, he would remember.

Olinka contemplates a jump into the sea from the high dive in Aden. (photo by Václav Hájek)

# Learning to Swim

$\mathcal{P}$acking for exile in 1949, Květa and Václav Hájek discreetly tucked baby Olga, affectionately and diminutively known as Olinka, into an air force parachute bag. They trusted her not to cry and as a trio escaped by foot through the Bohemian Forest for three days and three nights into Austria. After a few subsequent nights in a displaced persons camp, Václav made contact with the British who provided him and his family papers. As such, Václav, Květa, and baby Olga moved to England at 1949's end, and Václav re-joined the RAF. With the RAF, the trio moved to Scotland for a year in 1951, back to England in 1952, and later that year to Arabia.

Sixty-eight years later, Olga's unexercised memories present as patchwork. "I used to go by Loch Ness every day en route to school in Scotland. Every day I tried to see Nessie though never did," she recollects with a twinkle and a smile. "We theorized that there were actually multiple Nessies, once upon a time, but when the land masses shifted not enough Nessies remained in the Loch for mating purposes, and multiple became one, and one became none."

"I learned to swim in Aden. The brightly colored fish — that is how I remember the waters of Gold

Mohur. It was an officer's club. They had these huge nets to keep the sharks out. Then Steamer Point was the main town with shops and touristy bits. We were there for two and a half years. My dad was doing something with the RAF. We stayed in a beautiful standalone two-story house that felt three-story to me. I was so little and remember a huge spiral staircase. I remember the sand, miles of nothing, rolling nothing. My parents would let me go play. One day I was playing outside in the sand, and my mother snatched me up and whisked me off, without my sandals. There was not time to put on my shoes! Then the Queen went by in her convertible and waved at us especially. No one else was there. To a Brit, that is huge. Aden was a British Colony, and the new Queen was visiting the colonies. We had a cook, and a different person did each chore. My dad I suspect did not trust people there very much. We had a white dog named Pinkie and a black-and-white dog named Blackie, and some Arabs once poisoned steaks to kill the dogs then break into the house."

"For vacations we would go to Africa, Nairobi especially. I remember flowers and bees at that airport. The vegetation there was so different from that to which we were accustomed. We stayed at the Queen's hotel. I felt like a princess in that bed, with the diaphanous gauzy mosquito netting. Then we would go to game preserves to see the animals."

In 1954 the trio returned to England, this time to live in the village of Bitteswell before moving briefly to Maidenhead Road in Stratford-upon-Avon. Come November 1955, the family with one-way tickets boarded an ocean liner named Queen Elizabeth. "It had a full feeling on board the ship. We were down a deck or two from first class. Then we were in New York for a couple days, or maybe they were months," recalls Olga. The ship arrived in New York on 23 November 1955, and the family soon headed to Hollywood. By March 1956, Hawthorne Lane in Los Angeles became home, and Václav had submitted papers for the family's immigration and naturalization. Citizenship would take a while.

Did you ever feel like an outsider, as an immigrant, I asked her? "Well, I came over to the United States as a Brit. On the playground, if I said something, anything, all the kids would come over and circle around and want to hear me say it again. 'Say it again!' they would cry with glee. Was it mean? Oh, no, never. Once there was a spelling bee at Gardner Street School. I spelled a word wrong yet correctly in British English. 'Let her have it! That is not fair! Let her have it!' All the kids talked the teacher into letting me win."

# Pea Soup

When I was 4, Mom said we could go visit her friend who lived by the sea. The fog was as thick as pea soup, she said, as we hopped into the car. I loved pea soup. I played on the misty green lawn and waited for something thick and grand.

I remember being disappointed by the fog.

When I was 44 and spring had yet to arrive, snows began to melt in the night. Early morning raindrops pelleted city windows, but daylight savings be darned, we dashed through the morning waters, ducked into church, and heard in our hearts the gospel message of bread-broken Truth and wine-poured Grace. We headed home and rested while a great thick white fog enveloped our ivory tower from early afternoon well into the dark night. The earth was defrosting, and the air misted richly. It was a fog that made city buildings appear to disappear from sight.

"Baby," I said softly from the kitchen. He studied on the sofa after a supper of roasted eggplant, baked spaghetti squash fricasseed with tomato, garlic, and onion, and pan-seared butternut squash ravioli topped with fresh sage. Cooking soothes me. We were sipping an Italian red. His habit of bringing home inspired ingredients from which I could invent a meal had become our nourishing game, a felicitous foreplay of sorts, and our stay-in version of date-night out. "Will it bother you if I start the dishwasher?" He looked up at me with clear starry night eyes. "Darling, I am so in love with you, nothing can bother me."

I remember being grateful for the fog.

Olga Hajek

## A pretty mum, forsooth!

"If anyone says that the women of Shakespeare's town, Stratford-upon-Avon, aren't pretty, just show them this picture. It's of Mrs. K.A. M. Hayek [sic] and her six-year-old daughter Olga. They live in [sic] Maidenhead Road." ~Monday, 4 July 1955, *Daily Sketch*, p. 8.

Václav's 1954 photo of Květa with Olinka in Aden later wins £33s in the *Daily Sketch*'s Lovely Mother Series.

# Květa Kicks Off Correspondence

Los Angeles, 8 April 1959

ear Czech Family,

I have received your letter written on 30 March 1959 today. I was really happy, and I have to sit down and start writing. I have been planning that for almost two months.

We have received your letter with six photos, and you can imagine how glad we were. I inserted the photos in a glass frame and put them on a table. Olinka[1] hurried to try to learn who is who. Despite the fact she thought that Venda's[2] mummy is my mum and that the young grandpa must have been a film star because he is so handsome, she identified everybody. She tried to persuade me to let her take the photos with her to school.

In the evening it was the same surprise for Daddy. I had the feeling that it made him dizzy, and he roared at me in the kitchen: "For God's sake, where did you get them?" He had no idea that I had written you to send them to me. So now the pictures stand on a dresser in the bedroom, and we

---

[1] Olinka is the Czech diminutive for my mother, Olga.
[2] Venda and Vendí are affectionate references to Václav.

have a bit of our Czech home here. Thanks to God, we are all in good health, and I was happy to read that you were OK and that mum and auntie are healthy again, that Venouš[3] enjoys motorcycle to make it is easier for him to chase after girls.

The time passes, and we can realize that on Olinka when we see how she grows. Her broken left arm[4] is OK now.

About six weeks ago we bought a new piano, and Olinka has a piano teacher. The only difference from our old world is that here the teacher comes to our home. So each Thursday at 4 p.m., Olinka has a piano lesson. She likes it very much, and she plays immediately when she wakes up, but maybe it is just the beginning.

For two months we went to the mountains each Sunday where we enjoyed sledding and skiing. It is also possible to borrow everything including skis. But you have to go to 2000 meters or higher. Some hills are 3000 meters high, and it is impossible to get there by car. The only access is through the funicular. I remember how we went by the funicular to a hill, and we skied happily and then sat in the restaurant to eat some sandwiches, and we looked to the other side from Los Angeles to the

---

[3] Květa had a younger brother, Venouš.
[4] She broke it playing dodge ball.

Mojave Desert, which is flat as a table. From there people like to come here to cure flues, relax, and clean their bodies full of heavy air of the large city. Today there is some snow only at the tops of hills, but you can go for wonderful trips through the wild nature.

Next week we are planning to go to the sea as it becomes warm, and the weather in the mountains will be too hot and dry. It is not possible to bathe in the sea yet, but there is lovely salty wind there, and with a scarf on your head it is nice to walk there and play with a ball. I have to finish. I am looking forward to some news from you and send me, please, also Anča's address. I am sending best regards to all your friends and neighbors and best regards to Prague.

Yours,
Hájekovi with Olinka (the Hájeks)

~~~

Los Angeles, 19 July 1959

Letter N°1

To Miss Olga Hájek c/o Camp Osito-Ranch Girl Scout Camp at Big Bear Lake:

Dear Olga,

It is 2 p.m. on Sunday afternoon and we are sitting at home, little bit tired from yesterday and thinking of you. We miss you every minute, and do you know what we are doing to cheer us up? We repeat all good "jokes" you used to read, so we can laugh. Daddy cannot forget the one with the lady with that saxophone.

As I mentioned, we are tired from yesterday, so I am going to tell you where we have been. About 2 p.m. we decided to go swimming to NEWPORT BEACH, where we arrived about 3 p.m. I put my new swimming suit on, and we laughed because we felt all "blue." My swimming suit is blue, Daddy's suit is blue, our car is blue, and we thought that if you were with us at least your lips would be blue being too long in the water already.

We took a nice walk on the beach and then a swim. I enjoyed my first swim in the sea very much. Daddy was very nice to me, but he did not feel like playing ball, which by mistake I took with me completely forgetting that you were not there with us.

Later, after "dinner" in the car we took a walk on the pier where we saw fishermen being lucky catching little "SHOVEL SHARKS."

About seven o'clock we left to drive-in theater "LA MIRADA" where we saw "AL CAPONE." As you know, I don't care for those sorts of films, but Daddy was happy as an elephant. He bought me "HOT DOG" and "ROOT BEER" and later "HOT CHOCOLADE." Next film was something about "DEVIL" with Dan Murray, but we did not like it so left in the middle of it.

We came home after midnight and got up late in the morning. Now while sitting at the table writing this letter to you I can see "LINLEY" washing the car so I can see what a good example you set by helping Daddy the other day.

All seems to be very quiet over here, and I hope you are having a good time with children around the camp. We are looking forward to your letter, as it will be something to cheer us up.

Your loving,
Mum and Dad.

~~~

Los Angeles, 22 July 1959

Letter N°2

Dear Olga,

This morning we received your letter N°1. Thank you very much as we have been expecting that letter every day.

First thing I did is that I told to Sunny[5] about your new name in camp. She was jumping all over the cage, shouting "Olga-Sunny! Olga-Sunny!" so you see how happy she was.

We are happy to hear that you have got a nice tent and company. Letter N°1 I mailed to you on Sunday night and I hope you have got it already.

There is nothing new around here, only in the morning we had a little rain. Just a few minutes ago, "FRECKLES" was visiting us, and he got such a big dinner that he could not eat any more.

We are looking forward to your letter N°2 and hope it will tell us more about yourself.

God bless you.

Your loving,
Mum and Dad.

~~~

---

[5] "We had a little yellow parakeet. She was so cute, so smart, such a little person!" my mom recalls, 60 years later, when I ask her who was Sunny.

Los Angeles, 25 July 1959

Letter N°3

Dear Olga,

On Saturday morning we received your letter N°2, which we have been expecting every day. Thank you very much. It gives us little bits of ideas how you live, feel, and what you are doing. Your letter is from the second day in camp so we cannot tell too much from it, but we are sure that you are having fun being with children and we are happy for you, because of your change in daily life and that you are out of smog and noise of Los Angeles.

I really don't know what to write down from our daily ordinary life, nothing special happened. Daddy goes to work and I am retouching. Last two days are so hot we can hardly breathe.

One thing that is sure we are missing you very much you monkey, so I am sending you this little "handkerchief:"[6]

> *Three monkeys sat in a coconut tree, discussing things as they're said to be.*

---

[6] A square paper napkin illustrated with monkeys is tucked into the letter.

*Said one to the others, "Now listen, you two,*
*there's a certain rumor that can't be true — that*
*man descended from our noble race — the very*
*idea is a disgrace!*
*No monkey ever deserted his wife, starved her*
*babies, and ruined her life.*
*And you've never known a mother monk to*
*leave her babies with others to bunk,*
*or to pass them on from one to another 'til they*
*scarcely know who is their mother.*
*And another thing you'll never see — a monk*
*build a fence 'round a coconut tree,*
*and let the coconuts go to waste, forbidding all*
*other monks a taste.*
*Why — if I'd put a fence 'round a coconut tree —*
*starvation would force you to steal from me.*
*Here is another thing a monk won't do — go out*
*at night and get in a stew,*
*or use a gun or club or knife to take some other*
*monkey's life.*
*Yes, man descended — the ornery cuss — but,*
*brother, he didn't descend from us!"*

Sunny shouts at me to send you "HI," and Freckles barked at me to say you "RAF." We are looking forward to letter N°3.

Your loving,
Mum and Dad.

P.S. I hope you have got two letters already.

~~~

Big Bear Lake, 27 July 1959

Mr. & Mrs. V. Hájek,

Olga is a very enthusiastic camper as well as a very neat housekeeper.

She has taken the name of "Sunny" as her camp title and is making new friends rapidly.

Sunny misses home in the evenings but is becoming adjusted to camp life very well.

Sincerely,
Margo "Bugs" Alexander

~~~

Los Angeles, 28 July 1959

Letter N°4

Dear Olga,

I have not much time, but thank your leader "BUGS" for nice postcard. I am very proud of you being such a nice girl in camp.

Be happy every minute in the mountains because it is hot in Los Angeles.

I hope you will get this letter before you come home. We have got only two letters from you, but it is all right. We know you enjoy it, and we are proud of our Girl Scout.

We spent all weekend at home thinking of you, and we are looking forward to your jokes.

Bye, and see you soon.

Your loving,
Mum and Dad.

~~~

Los Angeles, 29 August 1959

Letter N°5

Dear Olga!

It's Saturday afternoon. I miss you very much everywhere but I am so happy for you being in the fresh air and out of the hot sun and smog of Los Angeles. I am sure you will find new friends over there again.

I am enclosing a card that came yesterday. I think it is very interesting for you, and you will understand better than I can.

> To Miss Olga Hájek c/o Glenn Shaw
> Agency, 8746 Sunset Boulevard:
> Please forward to 7271 Hawthorne Avenue:
> Please forward to 1408 N. Sierra Bonita:
>
> Bridgeport, Connecticut, 31 March 1959
>
> Dear Olga — Would you mind sending me an autographed photo? I think you are very cute!
>
> Sincerely,
> Robert M. Quinn

At home everything is all right. Daddy took me yesterday night out to dinner at a Viennese restaurant as special birthday treatment.

I would like you to see what I ate: Full half of goose with dumpling and cabbage. (Goose was not alive.) You can imagine that I am nursing my stomach all day today.

I think we are going to see the Pachls today, so Daisy can tell me how it is in the mountains. Then I will be able to figure out how you feel during the night and day.

I am looking forward to your letter.

Thousand kisses,
Your Mum and Dad.

~~~

Los Angeles, 3 September 1959

Letter N°6

Dear Olga!

I have received your letter. Thank you very much.

So you are in Rancho — good for you. I am very proud of you. Maybe you will come home much braver.

But only if you know how I miss you.

At home nothing happened since you left only one more new tooth in my mouth.

I am practicing piano too so poor Dick our teacher will have another headache besides you. I think he would be lucky to gain 10 pounds — he will need strong nerves.

We spent all weekend at home so I am sure you were lucky to be away. I hope you are not cold during the night; in that case you can wear sweater and socks.

So dear Olinko, I am looking forward to when you come home and to read your letters.

Thousand kisses.

From,
Mum and Dad.

Václav Hájek loves his Leica and takes a self-portrait with Květa. (photo by Václav Hájek)

# The Graveyard Waits

*A* heavy mist
Shrouds all but a few lonely objects
From view.
Here and there,
An ominous shadow is revealed,
Only to be swallowed up
Again
In the fog's drifting mouth.
The fog parts;
Moonlight illuminates
With its pale, chilling light,
Lending an unearthly glow
To the gloomy setting.
There
Exposed
An old stone cross,
Words worn away
By time,
Stands on a forlorn,
Weed-covered mound.
At a distance,
Partially engulfed by the mist,
Stands another,
Another,
And yet another.
It's quiet
Too quiet.
The silence oppresses,

As though the night
Were waiting,
Just waiting.

"The Graveyard Waits"
c. 1960, by Olga Marie Hájek

On 14 April 1961, Václav and his 13-year-old
daughter Olga became citizens of the United States.

# Václav Hájek Picks Up the Pen

Los Angeles, 25 May 1970

ear Father-In-Law,

Thank you for your letter that I received on 17 March 1970 together with a letter from my auntie. Before this letter, I received a letter that was enclosed with Zdenci's letter from 31 January 1970. I am glad that you like the enlarged pictures. When I look at these pictures, I realize what short skirts Olinka has. But it is a fashion here! But just in these days we can see the turn. Skirts and coats are longer than those of imperial officers. Bus drivers say it is wonderful because they will not have to sweep floors of their buses from dust and garbage. Nevertheless, short skirts still prevail in 98% because girls (and even older women) as well as nasty men love this fashion. The protectors of "long fashion" hope that they will win with the start of winter.

Not to breach the tradition, I have to start with my excuses and apologies that I have not written to you for a long time. Olinka was in Hawaii at Easter for about 10 days. She came back very happy. Next month she will graduate from Stanford University. If everything is OK, the festive graduation ceremony will take place on Sunday the 14th of June

1970. (I will go there.) The following day there is the tenth anniversary of that day when Květa passed away (15 June 1960 at six o'clock in the morning of the Pacific time.) When I look back I cannot believe it. Without Květa it was very, very difficult.

Olinka is beautiful after her mum and "eager beaver" after me! Now she graduates from the university, and she is "fed up" with books. She is not interested in getting married for "at least two more years." She likes traveling and meeting new people, and she would like to work abroad. But she does not like the idea to be stuck at one place, and so she came with an idea to work as a stewardess with the airlines for the next two years!! I got very angry which then confirmed her decision. So far this is her wildest plan, but I am sure she will think of something even wilder!

She has the smile of an Angel, and she is happy to do everything I do not agree with! When I drive our "Buick" on the motorway, I keep the maximum speed (about 105 km/hour). And she teases me that "parking" on motorways is strictly forbidden. When she drives, I better close my eyes and pretend that I am sleeping to avoid arguments between us two! Nevertheless, I am alert and from experience I know that when she starts to sing quietly and happily, we are driving at least 120 km/hour. She skis both in the mountains and on lakes behind motorboats. She rides a horse as a native Indian, and she climbs sharp mountains as a chamois. Only sometimes when it is dangerous do they use ropes.

Today I have received a letter from her with photographs, and my hands are still shaking!!! The pictures were taken at the Pacific coast to the west from the university. She is among a group of students—boys (and one girl) and she wears a diving suit and she smiles happily. The enclosed letter explains that it was a wonderful experience and I should not be afraid for her because before real diving she had several weeks of training with an expert in the university pools!

A few weeks ago she mentioned just by the way that she piloted a plane with students who learn that at the airport near the university!!

At the same time one fellow student explained to her at the university courtyard how to drive a racing car and then he let her drive (how stupid of him). And she went to the nearest motorway. Alone! She drove along the motorways and then a hand of gas manometer went to a zero! This took several hours and the frightened boy was glad when she came back with his machine! Since then she has been talking about our Buick as "a toy for babies."

I believe that these few examples explain my situation to you. I try to understand her more than in the past. It is the period when she feels independent, but she still comes to me to ask for advice or to tease me. It takes all my time to the extent that I stopped chasing wild cats in the mountains. I believe that Venouš will not have such troubles with his Olinka[7] as I have with "your" Olinka. If this is related to the name perhaps it is better that he stays single?!?!

The auntie writes nicely and legibly and her memory is excellent, full of details! For example, she writes of Hartman's recollections: "I remember that Květa talked about Vendí with an admiration and about Vendí's desire to 'achieve something,' and she admired Vendí's energy in overcoming language and social barriers."

Daddy, when I get some "ordinary" letters I usually read them in the evening in the kitchen while I prepare some "fast" food.

---

[7] Václav Mach's son Venouš, who was Květa's younger brother born in 1929, eventually married a woman 14 years younger than him named Olga. In 1971 the couple had a daughter also named Olga, and in 1972 they had a son also named Václav. Venouš is a pet form of the male given name Václav. Olinka and Olinko are affectionate forms of the female given name Olga.

But when I get a letter from you, I sit at my desk and look at the photographs of Květa, Olinka, and you, how you go out with a pair of horses from the gate!! When I read your words, and you almost always ask me to write something from my "history," I stop reading and have to look at Květa with a smile and she smiles at me. I have the feeling that we all warm each other with our smiles. This may seem foolish to you but I spend several hours at this desk pondering what and how to write to Olinka. After each line I raise my eyes and I ask Květa secretly what she would do. Sometimes my military nature does not agree with Olinka. But Květa never, really never, lost her Angel's patience, and therefore Olinka has got as far as where she is now. Many children here stray from their way. Olinka has achieved what one in a thousand of her fellow students achieves. She will not only finish the university, but Stanford selects from high schools the best ones of the best!!!

Květa gave Olinka all the best when she was small. I could not give her more than to continue in the started direction. I do it in such a way that I live with Květa in my thoughts in the present, and I try carefully to influence Olinka's life so that she does not damage her future.

And now about the past. I have not written the chronicle, despite your logic and good reasons. When it is possible, I would love to go home. If you agree, I would like to take my auntie to Ohnišov. We will get a barrel of good Czech beer and a chain of sausages. (There is a lot of meat here, but the smoked goods are terrible!) And if it is during the "season," Zákravský with Šubrt may know about a small piece of "extra" deer?! But this is only a fantasy and as I have already mentioned, I am looking forward mainly to sausages!

Everything will be OK with the chronicle! The auntie will help me, and I will eat and drink and as a veteran knock on the floor with my proverbially wooden leg and talk — I will talk and answer all your questions. And you will write everything you will want, OK? Explanation: My auntie often mentions a factory. This is because as a boy I was not good at studying. And therefore upon the advice of my uncle Rykl (he was also at our wedding) my parents gave me a lesson and it helped! (My auntie tried to console me.)

Maybe I am not answering some of your questions. Remind me of them again, OK? I really liked that Šubrt's idea with building a kennel — as an excuse and a place for drinks!

Send my best regards to all friends and to our hunters. Much success in hunting!

Yours,
Hájekovi (the Hájeks)

P.S. I have noticed from the post stamps that the mail from you is delivered in five to seven days. We fly to the Moon in four days, but mail from the U.S.A. takes 12 days to get to you!

When I got the last letter from you, you still had snow. When you get this letter, you will probably prepare for the harvest, won't you? However, this is my mistake, not post office's mistake. You can see, how quick I am in writing also from the crossed date. (Next time I will write the date after I finish the letter!)

~~~

Ohnišov, 5 June 1970

Dear Auntie,

Unexpectedly and finally we received a letter from Vendí. Read it first and we can talk about his news. He has troubles, but I think he does not take them too tragically and is in good humor. Twenty years have passed since they left the country, and he thinks that the life here is still the same when on the contrary; we do not have a clear idea about their life, and we do not understand those wild Olinka's ideas. The life there must be completely different from here, general prosperity that makes it possible to enjoy life – flying, racing, diving. We do not have an idea about these activities. Their society and circumstances enable that.

According to Květa, Olinka was very good at sports from her childhood. I remember how she wrote from Aden that Olinka jumps to the sea from a high jumping board to the admiration of all the others. She must take after her father. Not everybody has the courage to be a pilot, and when you get older you start to think about your life with more responsibility. As every other person does, we think about the time when we were young and admit we would not now repeat many of these activities.

I am not surprised that with such a busy life he does not have time to write. He has never mentioned his troubles with Olinka, and now she could die in a minute; therefore, he is afraid for her. I hope she is as lucky as he was when only three out of 14 pilots came back from the war. We will keep our fingers crossed on the 14th of June, and we will think about her.

What about you and your eyes? Write us about it, or let Zděnka do it. I want to respond to Vendí's letter within 14 days from when we received his letter, and I can enclose your letter too in order that he gets some fresh news from you. It is very cold here; spring has not started yet. There are still some blossoms on the apple trees, but lilac is not in full bloom, the sun does not shine too often, mostly it is cloudy, and there are showers. It seems impossible to fathom how we once had early cherries by mid-June.

Thank God we are well. Venouš is still single, and we hope that will end by summer so that he can bring the girl home and make it happier here. I am still busy because his Olinka wants a dog, which means we have to repair the fences in order for the dog to have a closed yard. We have not had a dog for 10 years, and I wanted a dog but Venouš did not. Now I look forward to it.

I am enclosing smaller pictures for Zdenička because Vendí initially sent us larger sized photos. I suggested smaller ones to him when I saw that he paid USD 1.20 on postage alone. Well, dear auntie, we have to stay healthy to see Vendí one day when he returns. I do not believe that Olinka will come with him when she is so wild. I am afraid that she is going to get herself killed. It would be better for her to get married and wise up, but it is in God's hands.

Best Regards to the Old and the Young and to You, Machovi (the Machs)

~~~

"Wild Olinka" jumps hurdles with the Stanford
Track Team pre-Title IX. (photos courtesy of Haack
family albums)

Los Angeles, 6 August 1975

Dear Father-in-Law,

Again I am in the same situation. I am planning to write a lot and then I postpone it. So now at least a few lines in order that you know that we are all right.

I received both your letters OK: The first one I received on the 4th February with a letter from Zdenička, two slides, nice Czechoslovak stamps on an envelope = hunting engravings and some stamps inside. The second one – on the 12th May with a beautiful stamp-motif from the 20th Olympiad.

An explanation of the group photo I am sending: It was taken about 11 months ago (at the end of August 1974). We drove 300 km by car with the young ones to visit Olinka's husband Tom's parents. Anička[8] was just 4 weeks old. You see Anička relaxed on a blanket. Above her — Tom's father Robert. He holds their dog "Andy" with his left hand. The dog was too curious and wanted to play with Anička in the manner that he usually plays with cats.

---

[8] Anička refers to me, Anne.

It is a small "panic." Everybody was afraid that he might hurt her. Tom's mother — Catharine — she is afraid that the dog will tear her tights and therefore she hides her legs in the armchair so is on her knees. To the right at the front — in red jumper there is Tom's sister Elizabeth.

"Cut" — completely on the right in blue trousers there is Tom's sister Barbara. At the back there is Olinka — in dotted blouse and she eats something from a bowl. On her left there is the "auntie Toni" — in colorful blouse without sleeves. Toni is the sister of Catharine's mother (one of three alive sisters of Catharine's mother.) Tom's mother Catharine, her mum died when Catharine was young and Toni then helped with her upbringing. (I sit under Olinka's left elbow.)

Catharine blamed Tom that he took a snap in such an unsuitable and unprepared moment. But it is like beating the air. He says to his mother that those natural pictures are the best ones! He does the same to Olinka — he always takes a picture when she is not ready. Then the female "victims" get angry, but after a while everything is forgotten.

Recently Tom and Olinka have bought their own house after the long and due consideration. (They paid the smaller amount in cash and they took a loan for the rest.) Tom likes gardening in his free time. Probably there is a lot of greenery around the house because Olinka calls it the "Paradise." They already have the most important furniture, and now they are buying the rest.

About a week ago it was Anička's first birthday. Besides "crawling" she tries to take her first steps. She has several teeth. She also likes to help her mum in the kitchen — she puts small things on their places. I talk to Olinka via the phone at least once a week across America. She seems to be happy and she cares for Anička with love as her mummy cared for her. I often hear many nice words about both of them from Tom's parents and sisters.

Olinka sometimes affectionately complains about Tom that when he comes back from work late he is too noisy (despite her reprehending) in order to wake Anička up and to have an opportunity to play with her.

Tom's family members sometimes offer advice on upbringing. Olinka very politely listens to them. But then she picks up the phone and asks, "Daddy, how did my mum raise me?" Seconds and minutes pass and I think and try to remember and explain. And how her mum did it — it is the law in their family — it must be like that!

It is raining a lot in the part of the country where Olinka lives. They have floods in the neighborhood. On the contrary here in South

California it is hot and dry (as each year). The vegetation in the mountains is dry, and there are often fires here.

If the fire bursts in an accessible place, the firemen try to localize it and extinguish with "old-fashioned" means.

If the fire bursts in an inaccessible place, they drop there specially trained firemen with parachutes and they pour water from helicopters and bombers that have been converted to tankers. We do not even notice if earthquakes accompany the fires.

My best regards to my best auntie. I often think of her! Thank you for both letters and a letter from Zdenička.

Best regards to the Zákravskýs, the Dusíleks and all hunters, relatives, and friends.

Best regards to small Olinka and Venoušek.

Yours sincerely,
Hájek

~~~

Ohnišov, 15 August 1975

Dear Zdena!

After a long time we have received a letter from Vendí, and I am sending a copy of the original for the auntie. But as usual he does not write too much and looking at his letters from the past I realize that he wrote more. Now we have to read more in between the lines as we have the feeling that he wants to stay anonymous for censors and due to his own safety. We have to forgive him because he knows this world better than we do, and I am really sorry that his desire to return to his country is so complex.

We think about the auntie. How is she? I want to answer his letter by 15 September so send me, please, some news for him about the auntie and all of you.

Best regards to the auntie and to all of you.

Yours,
Machovi (the Machs)

~~~

Ohnišov, 24 October 1976

To the esteemed Nyklíčeks family!

Let us condole you upon the death of our kind mum, mother-in-law, grandmother, and great grandmother. We deeply sympathize with you in your misfortune.

As my son-in-law deeply esteemed the auntie and liked her as his mother, we are sending him a funeral notice to keep it as a memory. We have not received any news since 28 December 1975, and I hope that after the receipt of this sad letter, he will write earlier than in the usual time around Christmas. After I receive some news from him, I will send you a copy of his letter as usual, because you are his closest relatives.

Best regards, I grieve together with you.
The Mach family from Ohnišov

~~~

Los Angeles, 28 November 1976

Dear Father-in-Law,

Thank you very much for your last four letters. I read them again and again. Please, accept my best regards, apologies, and excuses.

Daddy, in the letter from 14 December 1975 you mentioned the then-director of the school in Dobřany-Gerstner. It is interesting that after more than 40 years I immediately recalled a clever and young teacher. He was always a good organizer, teacher of singing in the cultural life at the school in Mladá Boleslav. Then he was transferred to Liberec, and I was transferred to Levice in Slovakia. If you have an opportunity, send him my best regards.

It is clear from the letter from 25 January 1976 that the hunters care well for animals. Those shoots of deer, hares, and pheasants are almost incredible.

In the letter from 12 July 1976 you sent me a nice picture of your Olinka and Venoušek and a very nice photograph of yourself! There was also an article enclosed from "Voice of the Revolution" about Czechoslovak pilots — "Ironclad Threat." Hájek that is mentioned in the article is a different one — Hájek — Bomber. I was a peashooter during the whole war. (Hájek in "Burning Wings" etc. — that was me.)

I received the letter from 24 October on 2 November 1976. It included a picture of your Olinka and Venoušek by the car and a funeral notice of the dear auntie Ješínová! I had hesitated a lot before I started to read your letter and open the funeral notice. I suspected what was inside! Despite the fact the auntie lived a long life[9] and the end

---

[9] Quite beautiful, Barbara Ješínová Hájek (b. 19 March 1889, d. 19 October 1976) rescued photos from apartments of those exiled over the war years. Her

might have been reasonably expected, I was really shocked by her death.

I would like to delight Zdenička, but I do not find suitable words. Nice words about the auntie on the funeral notice are pure truth!

I remember: I had a nice childhood and adolescence. I had very good parents and many uncles and aunts, nephews, and nieces. All of them were nice and kind people. I loved them all. But "Jewish auntie" was something special! My father's sister, Zdenička's mum, was always my best auntie, and for my mum — she was the nicest of the dear people.

We from Vysočany = father, mother and me — and they from Žižkov = auntie Betinka with Zdenči — visited each other often. It was not far, and when the weather was nice we went via Pražačka and Žižkov on foot. Each visit was a holiday for me. It was always happy. Nice memories.

I will always remember my auntie as I remember all other good people who have already left me.

---

husband Václav Ješina went missing in action 28 August 1914 during World War I. She was affectionately known as auntie Betinka.

Sometimes when I am alone I remember the words of a poet from My Country: "If you leave me, I will not die! If you leave me, you will die!"

Olinka and Anička came to visit me and spend the second half of July 1976 with me. I went to the "East" too and spent with them some weeks this November.

Both visits are unforgettable! I have also to complain: When I showed Olinka your last photograph, she was really enthused what a buck her granddaddy, that is her mum's father, was, and she took it from me saying she wants to keep this photo herself!!!

I am glad that you are OK. Thank you for nice Czechoslovak stamps by which you always enrich a letter, and you always insert some. Your Olinka and Venoušek are nice children and drollery can be seen in their eyes. I am sorry that I do not write too often. But letters home wake my memories, and they are still painful. I keep contact with people here in the U.S.A. by phone.

Daddy, I really appreciate your forgivingness. I do not write and you do not repine at me, do not blame me!!

Anička was 2 years old on 1 August 1976—the photo with Olinka by the sea is from that time. The one with a fur is probably younger. I remember you all when I look at the photographs. I remember the name days, which are not celebrated here.

During hunting season I remember our wonderful and unselfish hunters. They raise animals and create favorable conditions for them and then shoot them. Here the animals are taken care of by paid state forestry personnel, and the hunters then go and shoot.

They shoot at everything that moves. When I go to the forest for a walk during the hunting season, I consider it more dangerous than participation in the air battle of London!

Best regards to you, relatives and friends, and our hunters headed by Honza Zákravský.

Special regards to Zdenička in this sad and painful period following the loss of her mother, my auntie. I deeply sympathize with her. And Zdenčí may protest as much as she wants, but her mummy was as much my mummy as hers!!!

Yours,
Hájek

P.S. For Zákravský: I shoot just rarely and only at "varmints" = here we usually have wild cats in distant and narrow ravines—I shoot from a precise pistol. The maximum visibility is 5 meters. (Fence-time is nothing for me.) It means to sit quietly at least for half an hour. I am alert for several minutes. And then my thoughts usually go to Ohnišov! And then when that small (10-25 kg) "devil" comes to me, I get so scared that I miss it!!! These are such intelligent and prudent predators that even the Indians have plenty of stories about them.

~~~

Ohnišov, 19 December 1976

Dear friends!

After almost a year Vendí wrote us. I was afraid there might have been an accident, but fortunately everything is OK. We can only speculate about the reason of their silence because he wants to stay anonymous. If I imagine how lonely he is, I do not wonder that he uses the poet's words. It is difficult to guess what would have waited for him here, but fortunately he came back alive. This will one day be judged by history, but at that time we will not be in this world.

I copied those parts of the letter about our hunters he cannot forget, and it is interesting that four of those fellows still like to think about him. It was cold here for about four days, maximum minus seven degrees Celsius, about 20 cm of snow fell but now it is above zero and just half of the snow is left, and it is wet.

Merry Christmas to all of you, to the young and old, and a happy new year.

Yours,
Machovi (the Machs)

~~~

Los Angeles, 15 March 1982

Dear Daddy,

Thank you for your thick letter from 8 February including a letter from Zdenička, 47 pages of the "Diary of My Grandchildren," a picture of Venouš' family, and slides of my home and school.

I received everything OK on Monday 22 February 1982.

I read the whole "Diary" several times — usually in the evenings. These are nice records and when I read them alone, I had the feeling as if I had been there with you!

The family picture shows that children are well. Olinka and Venouš can be proud of them! Your small Olinka reminds me of my Olinka when she was the same age!

My Olinka and I are too far from each other — across America. We give a call to each other once a week and visit each other twice a year.

The young are near the coast. In summer they are on the beach whenever they can be. Both Anne and Catharine (Kati)[10] can jump into the water from a jumping board, and they can swim very well. This winter Tom started to teach Anne cross-country skiing. When they do not have any snow, they can go north to the mountains.

Older Anne is very hard working and ambitious; she studies well. Kati is an adorable pet. She takes everything with humor, and nothing can make her angry; Olinka still believes that she will be like her mum (Květa).

It is nice to talk with Anne via the telephone, and she is very polite. When I talk to Kati, she gets bored very soon, she laughs and runs away and cries, "Mummy, Grandpa Hájek!" and she gives her the receiver and leaves to play.

---

[10] Kati is the Czech diminutive for Catharine, my sister.

I know I should write more, but I still believe that once I get home is when we will be able to talk personally a lot. I am still single, and I work.

Many regards to all of you, to all relatives and friends.

Yours,
Hájek

P.S. Once again thanks to Venouš for the picture of his family and Zdenička for two pictures from Vysočany.

~~~

Ohnišov, 18 April 1982

Dear Friends,

Finally we have received a letter from Vendí and it is for the first time when it took the whole month before we received it. I thought that Vendí made a mistake in the date, but really there is the date of the 15th March on the stamp. It is difficult to judge whether it was purposeful due to the Communists. I reminded him last time to write something for the family from his war experience, but he cannot find courage to do it.

We are OK here but await spring. Now it is afternoon and the sun is shining, but in the morning it was snowing and everything was completely white for a while. Winter has bothered us for too long.

I will answer his letter in summer and if you, Zdena, have any news from your family, write it and I will send it to him. Or you can visit me when you come to the Orlické Mountains while I am still alive.

Best regards to you and to all your family.

Yours,
Machovi (the Machs)

~~~

Los Angeles, 10 December 1982

Dear Daddy,

Thank you for your letter from 26 September, a photograph of children in the front garden, and nice Czechoslovak stamps. I received everything on 4 October. We are all OK and we see each other about twice a year but at least once a week we get calls to each other.

At the beginning of December there was unusual weather in South California for about three days. Storm came from the Pacific — Hawaii. Storm = rain and strong wind of up to 80 miles per hour (about 120 km/hour). Everything was flying! Roofs, trees, and all other things not anchored to the ground. There was an outage of power supply. High waves washed many villas into the sea (from beaches).

My only damage was a broken and torn umbrella! And now it is quiet again as usual.

Best regards to all of you.

Yours,
Hájek

P.S. Your Olinka and Venoušek in the photo are very nice.

~~~

Ohnišov, 23 January 1983

Dear Friends,

First I would like to apologize myself for a delay, but after many years I got ill. On 26 December I got a temperature 39 degrees Celsius. On 27 December my son took me to the doctor who did not find the reason of the fever. I got penicillin, and on 31

December I discovered that my left leg is almost dead. The doctor prescribed pills against vein inflammation, and it helped. In about three days swelling went away, the doctor prescribed antibiotics, I lost the fever, and then I got new pills to help my blood circulation. But I took the first pill and again — I got the temperature, and I was not able even to dress myself. So I do not take them. I do not know what the doctor will tell me, but I believe that I will overcome this disorder.

In the autumn we ordered a book <u>Magic Hawaii</u> and as my son-in-law writes about the storm, the author of the book also writes about storms. They are caused by the submarine volcanic activity and the death wave can be as high as 40 m. It moves very fast to the coast and damages everything — people, houses — and takes everything to the sea including parked cars. There were three catastrophes — in 1868, then shortly after World War II, and most recently in 1960. At that time the radio already warned people. But despite that, many people disappeared, and damages in the amount of millions were caused.

Zdenička, I will wait until the 15th whether you have any important news for Vendí from your family. Best regards to you and the young ones.

Yours,
Machovi (the Machs)

~~~

<div align="right">Los Angeles, 12 September 1983</div>

Dear Daddy,

Thank you for both your letters.

The first one — from 14 February — I received it on 23 February 1983. It contained also a letter from Zdenička, a letter from the Zákravskýs, and six nice Czech stamps. The second one — from 26 June — I received it on 6 July 1983.

I thought a lot about what to write for your "chronicle" about my military service, but the activity of our pilots abroad was described in several Czech books, and everything I could write about myself would sound as my "boasting." We all did what was possible, and many of us gave their lives.

But I still hope to get home sometime, and on that occasion you will have an opportunity to ask anything you want to your satisfaction — I promise that to you!

I am still single: ("No woman is such as Květa Machová"!!)

I still work full-time. I could retire, but I try to postpone it.

This year it has been unusually and unbearably hot here since June. It is tiring!

Tom and Olinka's family is OK. Both girls are good at school. Older Anička is the best in her class, and younger Kati is still a pet. Both learn to ride a horse. We telephone each other across America at least once a week.

I am writing in order for you to know that I am still alive. I am sorry, but I hope that we will have an opportunity to talk personally! I will write more once the weather gets colder! The oldest family member — a great grandfather Haack — died on 4 July 1983 in the age of 93.

Best wishes to all the Václavs — on the occasion of their name day on 28 September.

Thank you Daddy once again for everything, thanks to Zákravský for his nice letter about Ohnišov hunting and hunting stories.

Best regards to all of you, to all relatives and friends.

Yours,
Hájek

~~~

Ohnišov, 25 September 1983

Dear Friends,

Finally after three quarters of a year, Vendí wrote me a letter. Now he writes more about his visit to Czechoslovakia. I wish he could manage to come, as I would like to meet him while I am still alive. We would learn more about what he does.

There is nothing new here, thank God we are all healthy, and we hope you are also well. The time passes so quickly, and on 1 November I will be 90 years old. Children go to school and are almost as tall as me. The old age bothers me as my legs and backbone get weaker. In January I was ill with an inflammation of veins, and they cured me with pills; however, there are no pills against age.

The whole summer was very dry, and even in the water pipes there was not enough water. This has never happened before.

I would like to answer Vendí's letter, and I will wait 14 days. So if you, Zdena, have any news for him send them to me, please.

Best regards,
Machovi (the Machs)

~~~

Los Angeles, December 1983

Dear Daddy,

Thank you for your nice letter and insertion from Zdenička and nice Czechoslovak stamps. I received everything OK on 5 December 1983.

Merry Christmas and a Happy New Year to all the Machs, relatives, and friends!

Yours,
Hájek

~~~

Ohnišov, 1 January 1984

Dear Friends!

I am sending you a copy of the brief Christmas card. I do not understand the brevity. You don't think he wants to surprise us by visiting us as he mentioned last time, do you? I remember that he is 70 years old and maybe he asked for the retirement. He promised to write more about himself in September when it is not so hot, and so far we have not received anything. It is difficult to blame him as we do not know his personal situation, and moreover we have to bear in mind his responsible service. Nothing else can be done. We can just wait and hope. I would like to talk to him when I am still alive and to write something from his life in order that my grandchildren will remember him.

Here it is almost spring, but there is a proverb "green Christmas, white Easter" and this year the Easter is as late as 22 April. But if you look at what winter is in America, it is possible that it will come also here. And after that hot summer we can expect a tough winter in order that the annual average gets balanced.

Best regards to all of you.

Yours,
Machovi (the Machs)

~~~

Los Angeles, 10 December 1984

Dear Daddy,

Thank you very much for your letter, five Czechoslovak stamps, and a nice postcard from Ohnišov. I received everything OK.

We are all OK. Both Olinka's daughters are good at school.

I do not write too much, but we think about you a lot.

Once again thank you very much.

Yours,
Hájek

~~~

Ohnišov, 30 December 1984

Dear Friends,

On 30 August I sent him the letter with a request to reply within a month whether he has received it, but I waited in vain. I received these few lines as late as now. I am glad to hear they are well, but it is a mystery for us why he does not reply and if he does reply, then only just a few lines. Their life is very different from ours, he takes a lot of responsibility in his service, and under permanent pressure between west and east it is difficult to guess the reason. Once I asked him to write me something from his life for the whole family to remember him. But he answered that it would be boasting and he hoped to come to his home country one day when he could tell me everything, and then I can write about him. Now he is silent, and the time passes so quickly. On 1 November I was 90, and I cannot believe that I will live too long. Thank you for the Christmas card. Happy New Year to the whole family.

Best,
Machovi (the Machs)

~~~

Los Angeles, 11 December 1985

Dear Daddy,

Thank you very much for two letters, family photos, and nice Czech stamps. I am really sorry that I am too lazy to write letters! I do not write too often, but I think about you a lot!

We are all OK and in good health. I am still single, and I still work.

Again I am very sorry. Best regards.

Yours,
Hájek

Ohnišov, 27 December 1985

Dear Friends,

We have not received any news from him for the whole year and now just a few lines. I think that he is not too lazy to write but rather he is responsible in his service at the radar station. Frequent correspondence to Bolshevik Czechoslovakia could be dangerous for him under today's pressure between west and east. Even unknown postal stamps on the envelope prove that. We will learn the truth once he comes to Czechoslovakia. I do not think I will see him because I have turned 92. Such secret interstate matters cannot be described in letters. We have to hope that everything will get better, but the main thing is that they are all well. The Christmas is without snow, the temperature is around zero, and we are in quite good health. Zdenička, if you have any news from our relatives, write them for him. I will wait with a response until mid-January. When you come to Nové Město, come to visit us in Ohnišov while I am still alive. Thank you for the Christmas card.

Yours sincerely,
Machovi (the Machs)

~~~

Los Angeles, 15 December 1986

Dear Daddy,

Best regards to all of you and to all relatives.

Merry Christmas and a Happy New Year.

Thank you for two letters and a nice photograph of your Olinka and Venoušek.

Yours,
Hájek

~~~

Ohnišov, 5 January 1987

Dear Friends,

For a year we have not received any news but these few lines — however I am not surprised considering his responsibility and today's pressure between west and east. It is better to be silent. I am sorry he does not receive all letters from us. He thanks me just for two letters, and I have sent him four, and it is likely that he did not receive the fifth one from 6 December yet. All this can be explained personally when he comes to visit Czechoslovakia. However I do not believe in that. I will be 93 years old, and according to the Mach's family tree all men died at this age. Just one woman lived to 99, but women are stronger. Winter started here as late as at Christmas. By the end of the year it got warmer, and it is snowing now. If you, Zdenička, have any more important news for Vendí from other relatives, send them during January. I am going to write him at the beginning of February so that he has continuous contact with us. Thank you for your Christmas card.

Best regards.

Yours,
Machovi (the Machs)

~~~

Ohnišov, 28 March 1988

Zdenička,

Write, please, a letter to Vendí, and I will send it further. If he comes home by chance, I want for him to have fresh news about you in Prague. I have received the promised letter at Christmas.

Yours,
Machovi (the Machs)

# California to Connecticut I

In late summer of 1989, my mother went back to California to visit her father. He was not sick; he was just not able to function very well anymore at home in Los Angeles. She wanted to pack up his belongings and move him home or at least nearer to us in Connecticut.

My mom had asked my dad if he would be OK with us kids while she was west. It was around Labor Day weekend and in the midst of junior varsity field hockey season. I remember I had had four wisdom teeth recently removed.

Dad is a great cook and awesome father albeit a man's man. He grilled filets and steamed corn-on-the-cob. I remember trying to chew with my front teeth and missing Mom.

# California to Connecticut II

Westlake Village, 7 March 1990

$\mathcal{M}$ilá Olinko,

It was so nice to hear from you this morning. You are a beautiful human being, and it was such a pleasure to have you with us. We wish you could have stayed longer to enjoy the beauty of California all over again.

We are glad that you were able to relocate your father and keep an eye on what is happening. Your dad is a unique, one of a kind person unsurpassed by anyone I know. He is a man of honor, decency, loyalty, truthfulness, integrity, and thought. I have known him to be generous to a fault with impeccable old world manners, which he never abandoned. For his outspoken manners everyone might not have loved him, but he most certainly has still the respect of all who know him. He is truly a noble man; high-principled, selfless, caring, incorruptible; a true thoroughbred. Yes, he is opinionated, but he forms his beliefs after giving situations careful thought and then, right or wrong, he doesn't compromise.

Olinko, you can be very proud of your dad. Even today he holds his head up high. Above all, he doesn't like to be treated like a doddering old fool. He might be feeble but is not feebleminded to the point that he wouldn't understand that he is not being treated with the respect he earned and deserves. Olinko, make sure he gets it, and I am sure he will give back in kind.

It is very thoughtful of you, Olinko, and Tom, to send us a present 'in appreciation of whatever we did,' but it wasn't really necessary. Seeing you, Olinko, again, and getting to know your wonderful husband was a gift in itself. Every time I open the books you gave me, I think of you. Your daughters are truly blessed to have such concerned and decent and WISE parents as you both are.

Thinking of you with love in heart and wishing you the best.

Irma and Joe Séda

P.S. I'll write more often as soon as I learn how to handle the computer more efficiently. Next time I'll tell you what I know of a beautiful lady, Olinko: YOUR MOTHER.

~~~

Westlake Village, 10 March 1990

Milá Olinko,

Now that I examine my 'work of art' I wish I hadn't used the computer. Please excuse the format and all other inadequacies and just concentrate on the content.

To our conversation on the phone I would like to comment that it was I who learned from you. You provoked thoughts I didn't think before. Whenever worries try to spoil my day, your philosophy comes to the rescue and they often vanish. I quote you quite often. Whatever we put out creates a ripple effect and affects more lives than we can imagine. I got more from you, Olinko, than I could ever give you. You were a godsend. God bless you.

Please, Olinko, keep in touch. I know you don't like to write, so call once in a while, if that's possible.

Give a hug from us to your dad, Tom, and your beautiful daughters.

We love you,
Irma and Joe Séda

~~~

Westlake Village, 21 March 1990

Milá Olinko and Tom,

Thank you for the smoked salmon. What a wonderful, thoughtful gift. It arrived at the end of last week, but we haven't tasted it yet. I bet it's delicious.

Olinko, there isn't a day that I wouldn't reminisce and wonder, how you, your dad, and the rest of your family are doing. Your dad is so blessed to have a caring daughter and son-in-law, and your children as well, to have in you an example of what true love and concern are all about. I know that with your help and the help of God your dad will live out his life in peace. He was, and still is, a remarkable man. Your mother, Olinko, would be so proud of you. Your ways of thinking and conduct are admirable. You have our deepest respect.

A little rain in February resplended California to its usual brilliance of the spring season. The brown is replaced by lush green, flowers and trees are in full bloom, and our Bambula and Bambulina are busy collecting twigs for their nest and courting each other. We feel good in our little paradise.

Often I think of your mother, Olinko. You remind me of her. Květa was a beauty not only of looks but of heart as well. In me she left a lasting impression, although I knew her only for a short time. She had a down-to-earth, honest, unpretentious personality, real and natural. She was loving and loyal, well educated, and naturally bright. She evidently loved stylish clothes, and I always saw her impeccably dressed. Your dad and your mother were perfect for each other. They shared values neither of them would have ever compromised. They lived for each other and for you. I am sure that even in death she is with you in spirit and is guiding your life. Your dad was right. Your mother would have been hard to replace. She was a combination of strength and gentility; she possessed a delightful sense of humor and love of life, coupled with much common sense and decent values. As soon as I get organized I'll translate her life's story that is mostly represented by her letters she wrote to her parents.

What I truly regret is that your dad can't fully comprehend what is going on in his land of birth. We still are dumbfounded by all those remarkable developments. He would have liked President Havel's philosophy, telling his nation quite truthfully that not all of its ills are the fault of the Communists. Havel never surrendered his conscience to dictates of Communism, nor did he lie to his nation after he was elected. His message that the nation had become morally ill was a sobering thought, not too flattering but truthful. My thoughts on this are that hopefully the Czechoslovakian nation will recognize that freedom's immediate gift is to the soul, and economic success will take patience and effort. The possibilities there are endless if the stagnant nonsense of yesteryears can be overcome. They'll have to go back to the unfashionable virtues of hard work, hard study, saving more, and investing more. I pray to God the nations now free have the wisdom to recognize the value of freedom and are willing to pay the price.

I see that I have made a mess of this page but hope you won't mind if I don't rewrite this letter. I don't think you would get it in the near future.

Over Easter we'll have all three grandsons with us. They'll fly down from Reno all by themselves. I am nervous about the flight.

Give our love to your dad.

Love to you all!

The Sédas

~~~

Westlake Village, December 1990

Dear Olinko, Tom, and Family,

There isn't a day that I wouldn't think of you and wonder how you are. Olinko, how is your dad coming along? Any improvements, setbacks, or is everything the same? We are glad he is near people who love him and are genuinely concerned about his well-being. I know, Olinko, what a heartbreaking situation this is for you, but your belief in God's will may lighten the load.

How are you, Tom, and your lovely daughters? I have learned so much from your faith. Often, when I am worried, I put my burden into God's hand and miraculously everything gets resolved. As you can see, your spirit is still with me, and I hope we too have helped you to see some things from another point of view. Otherwise, we all are well and caring for each other. We love you, and we wish you and your loved ones the very best.

Merry Christmas to you all!

Lovingly,
The Sédas

~~~

Westlake Village, December 1991

Dear Olinko, Tom, and Family,

I hope all of you are in good health and good spirits. I am thinking of you often and praying that God give you the strength to cope. How is 'Grandpa' doing? He is so very lucky, in spite of his misfortune, to have a loving and caring family. God bless you all!

We had quite a year. After 42 years of 'exile,' we returned to the land of birth. We tearfully visited graves and lovingly embraced relatives still living. Czechoslovakia itself we could hardly recognize. The once clean, sparkling cities looked gloomy and uncared for, and the once high-spirited, gifted, and self-sufficient people were turned into a 'what-can-I-get-out-of-you' nation. Of course, there are some exceptions. The estate of my husband's family has been parceled off for housing—land and forests neglected! We were glad to come back 'home' to the U.S.A.

Shortly after our homecoming Julie's husband Steve and two of their sons were in a major car accident: Head-on collision with a drunk guy who crossed a double. They are recuperating, but it shook us all up, to say the least. Our granddaughters and grandsons are our pride and joy.

May your Christmas be overflowing with happiness, and may God bless you and keep you well. Love you all!

The Sédas

# Irish Cliffs and Wilton Meadows

$\mathcal{O}$t was not until my junior or senior year in high school that I deduced cross-country as providing the biggest bang for the buck in terms of athletic intensity and succinctness of time spent at practice. School was stressful in the self-imposed sense, and there seemed not enough hours in the day to get everything done before starting all over the next. An extra hour or two off the field was worth spades. Also, my Irish-from-Ireland friend Karen was living in the States for a few years, loved long runs, and seemed like one of the nicest people in the world.

One afternoon we had a cross-country meet up in Wilton. We had extra time at the meet, and I told Karen that my Czech grandpa now lived at a home across the field. She enthused we ought to run over and say hi, which we summarily did. He received us in his La-Z-Boy and later waved goodbye out the window. I remember glancing back at his twinkling blue eyes as we ran back to the meet.

Meanwhile, our coach departed with our backpacks in his van thinking that we were getting a ride home with someone else. This stressed me out to no end because I had so much homework to do. We ended up getting home and getting our backpacks a couple hours later; still, these were the days when every minute mattered.

Twenty-five years later Karen was back in Ireland and met an Irish guy, first while lighting memorial candles in a cathedral and then serendipitously again while running the cliffs. They dated and got engaged and wanted a small intimate wedding in Italy, because…Italy! Nuptials were on a Friday in Castelli Romani just outside Rome. I flew in a day early and sat sipping a Cesanese on my iron-wrought balcony overlooking the Frascati town square. Seventy-four years plus a day ago the town had been bombed in an Allied air raid ironically the same day that General Eisenhower announced the Allied armistice with Italy.

Karen's father and her 98-year-old grandfather together walked her down the aisle. We marveled particularly at how the latter had stayed alive to pray her through this marriage. Theirs was a warmhearted charismatic Catholic ceremony — I had not even known that sort of ceremony existed. They said the grandpa was completely deaf, but when I went to pay respects at the reception and to say how wonderful God is to have heard his prayers — "thank God for praying grandfathers" — he seemed to hear perfectly and smiled broadly with a knowing twinkle in his eyes.

# Ichthys

$\mathcal{D}$ad used to do work with China in the 1980s, and Mom accompanied him at least once or twice. Eventually one of their Chinese business friends helped arrange for our family of four to visit the country in 1992. I had just graduated from high school and was Stanford-bound in the fall. We wanted to experience the Yangtze River before purported construction began on the Three Gorges Dam.

Memories of this trip entail Dad encouraging Mom, my sister, and me frequently only to drink beer, because the bottled water when not sparkling was suspect. I remember we ate Peking duck in Beijing. I remember in the second or third week of the trip experiencing deep food cravings and comparing notes with my sister: Green crunchy apples and a bottle of cold seltzer water = mine; Ben & Jerry's Cookie Dough ice cream and a Diet Coke = hers. The persecution felt acute.

The bigger memory is more of an archetype, and it entails the ichthys. On a previous trip to China when Mom tagged along with Dad, they had met people who were not allowed to express faith. That Communism reigned not only in Czechoslovakia but also in China fascinated me. That people in today's world could be persecuted for faith or religion startled me; I had known it intellectually yet not viscerally. One of these people drew the top part of an ichthys in the earth, and Mom or Dad completed the bottom. Mom and Dad sowed seeds in this manner. Early Christians experienced persecution by the Holy Roman Empire, and drawing this fish symbol in the earth was a means of helping to discern friend from foe.

~~~

Xi'an, People's Republic of China, 23 July 1992

Dear Olga,

When you receive my letter, you may already have gotten that tiger screen which has been mailed on 16 July. The postman told me it would take one week or 10 days to get to your home. I hope Anne can get it on her birthday.

Olga, I'm sorry to tell you the postage to the States is very expensive. But Olga, you needn't mail money to me. You said you'd mail a Bible to me. I'll be very glad to get it. Thank you!

Your new friend,
Lily

# Olympic Landing

*I* wanted to go on a mission trip to Barcelona this same summer of 1992 after we got home from China, less for reasons of sharing the gospel and more because I wanted to go to the Olympics. I applied for the Barcelona trip and ended up getting accepted on a mission to Moscow and Saint Petersburg instead. The dissolution of the U.S.S.R. had just occurred in December of 1991, and the trip proved tremendous.

Miraculously, despite language limitations, our spiritual warrior gang of 15 had at least doubled by trip's end. We performed street skits to provoke wonder without words, and curious crowds would grow. My favorite skit was one with me praying, on my knees and looking up prayerfully to the sky, while dramatic battle music played and two big Michigan dudes whom I was not supposed to notice or get distracted by did a sword fight all around and over me. The battle belonged to the Lord, was the point. My role was to praise and trust Him radically and completely.

I remember buying a water painting at Red Square on the black market in dollars, for seven one dollar bills to be exact, and the artist and I both won in that transaction. The amount of rubles one could get for a dollar would nearly quadruple by the time we departed, and the timelessly exquisite and colorful painting still hangs on my wall today.

Our core group upon return got hung up at passport control in Moscow, and I remember feeling acutely stressed because if we did not make the flight I might get home to Connecticut too late to get to U2's Zoo Tour on Saturday night. Then that prayer posture tickled my heart. The battle belonged to the Lord. We made the Aeroflot flight.

When we landed at JFK, our families and friends at arrivals acted beyond relieved because apparently an Aeroflot plane had crashed or exploded while we were in the air, and the news reporting had been unclear as to the fact that it was a different Aeroflot flight, a domestic one, that had gone down. (Later I learned that domestic flights do not need to meet international flight regulations.) I continue still to offer up prayer and praise at lift offs and landings.

# Valedictions and Salutations

𝒪n 1 January 1993, Czechoslovakia ceased to exist. It had peacefully divided into two nations, the Czech Republic and Slovakia. I remember a mournfulness in my mom that New Year's Day.

~~~

Salem, Oregon, 20 September 1993

Dear Tom and Olinko,

I hope you do not mind me calling you Olinko! That's what we all called you at the time! And it was the happiest time of my life! I could hardly wait for Saturday — and, then, we all went to Newport Beach, later on to Ghost Town at Knott's Berry Farm — and, then, to the Drive-In Movie.

On the way home (around 2 a.m.) we followed one another on the freeway and honked to say, "Good night!" when our ways separated. You cannot even imagine how happy your call has made me!

Our families were the best of friends — I guess, we were replacing to each other the relatives we left behind in Czechoslovakia-Bohemia. Your mother was beautiful (I'll try to find some pictures), and your father helped me through the most difficult times of my life — God Bless Him!

Please, stay in touch, give my best to your father, and call me "BABI" (grandmother in Czech). I could be Babi to your daughters — your mom and I are the same age!

Love,
Babi Kurka with Vita and Mitzi (my two puppies)

~~~

Svit, Slovakia, 7 July 1995

Dear Mr. And Mrs. Haack, Anne, and Kati!

I would like to send you my best regards from "Czechoslovakia." Coming home, meeting my family and friends, traveling around a little bit have killed my first three weeks since I left my America.

Meeting my parents and my brother was AWESOME, I can't express it in other way. All of us have changed a little bit but as far as I can see, these changes seem to be rather positive. You were right when you said that I would see how much I changed especially when I came home. The way of talking, the relationships, the attitudes, the knowledge, everything makes me seem a little older. In general though, not a lot of things altered that drastically. People who were my real friends stayed that way, the ones who were 'morons' before stayed the same as well. The only thing that bugs me now is the fact that because I was in the U.S., a lot of people don't stop criticizing me no matter what I do. Well, if that should bother me, I would have to admit how weak I am. And after Deerfield, nobody, not even me, stays weak.

OK now something interesting: Due to the fact that everybody in my school and my family, including me, is eager to see me graduate in '97 instead of '98, I will be studying for special exams. If I pass them, I'll be able to join my old class and continue in my German education. Whatever might happen in the future, the plan for next year is clear. I will be living alone in the mountains in Slovakia. We have our old apartment there, and I will be studying hard and taking care of myself. Considering that my friends from school will be close, it's not that bad. And trip to Brno takes 'just' eight hours.

Finally, I would like to tell you that I 'started' my research about the history of your family. All I know so far is that Ohnišov exists but is probably so small that I haven't even found it on the map of Czech Republic. Fortunately, my father has a degree in geography and has promised me that we would try to find more information soon. In case that the village is pretty close to where we now live, he would actually be willing to drive me there. I can't promise too much yet, but if the time slows down a little, I will be able to dig into it.

I wish you all a great summer, lots of sun, lots of water, and tons of energy for being such wonderful people as you unquestionably are. It's hard to be nice (sometimes), but it doesn't cost anything. As with a box of chocolates, you never know what you get. But sometimes, as with meeting you, one gets just the right chocolate, the one one likes the most!!!

With love and respect,
Your Daniela Veverková

# Silver Anniversary

$\mathcal{O}$n 1996, Tom and Olga flew to Prague for their 25th wedding anniversary. They found where Václav Hájek had lived while he was in the Czech Air Force. A 50-meter high statue of Stalin had been unveiled out front in 1955, destroyed in 1962, and recently replaced by a 32-foot one of Michael Jackson for the HIStory World Tour.[11]

~~~

Darien, Connecticut, December 1996

To all of our Friends:

As you gather with family and friends this Holiday Season, we wanted to share a very personal, heartwarming family event in our lives. To celebrate our 25th wedding anniversary this past September 11, we journeyed to the Czech Republic, Olga's birthplace. This was particularly significant because, as a baby, Olga left Czechoslovakia in her father's parachute bag as her parents escaped political persecution by fleeing on foot through the frontier borders into Austria. Olga has never been back to her homeland, and, in fact, has never had

---

[11] https://www.pophistorydig.com/topics/the-jackson-statues-1995/

any contact with her relatives in the Czech Republic.

As somewhat of an afterthought to our deciding to visit the Czech Republic, we thought it might be interesting to try to find Olga's relatives. Armed with only several very old photos of the farm on which Olga's mother grew up, the name of the town, Ohnišov, where the family had lived, and the family surname, we drove early on a Sunday morning 160 kilometers from Prague into northeastern Bohemia to where we thought Ohnišov was located. At our destination, a picturesque village that was, indeed, Ohnišov, our first stop was the church set atop a small hill. We intended to query parishioners as to their knowledge of the Mach family, but everyone had already left. As we walked back from the church to the car, however, Tom noticed a very distinctive barn structure about ¾ of a mile across the valley, which apart from increased foliage appeared identical to the farm in our photos! Within minutes, we were in the driveway of what definitely had been Olga's mother's farm.

Olga nervously knocked on the door, and, as an elderly man and woman answered, Olga started to say in her semi-fluent Czech, "My name is Olinka Hájeková, and my mother grew up on this farm." Before even completing this introduction, the man and woman started wildly hugging Olga and crying: They were Olga's uncle and aunt! Even our driver was in tears. The uncle, who was Olga's mother's younger brother and now 67, had last seen Olga 48 years ago when he was a teen and Olga an infant. Within minutes, Olga's two cousins and niece arrived, and the reunion reminiscences proceeded in free flow.

With warmest regards,
Olga and Tom

# Non-Existence v. Persecution

$\mathcal{F}$urther investigation during this visit led to a profoundly delightful meeting with Major General Karel Mrázek, then 86. General Mrázek as a famous Czech freedom fighter had commanded Václav Hájek when they flew together during WWII. General Mrázek told Tom and Olga that Václav had indeed made the correct decision to defect: When the Communists were in power, the role of the WWII Czech pilots was something the Reds wanted suppressed.

For 40 years, in Czech history books, the air force of General Mrázek and Václav Hájek did not exist. Their contributions as part of the Czech, French, and British forces were never acknowledged. Moreover, fellow officers who stayed but did not embrace the Communist ideology were politically persecuted. Those who insisted on remaining usually found themselves either in menial jobs, unemployed, or arrested.[12]

Olga entered Stanford University in 1966 and hoped to return to the European continent with the undergraduate overseas program. In 1968-1970, the

---

[12] Sourced from a rough draft paper copy of <u>Olga's Story</u>, by Olga Hájek Haack class of 1970, as told to Tod Tolan, class of 1971 for Stanford 2000 Reunion materials.

political scene in Czechoslovakia was particularly volatile. Although Olga was not informed at the time, her application to the German and Austrian Stanford campuses was rejected because of concerns for her personal security. By her senior year, it was too late to meet the language requirements for Italy or France.

The Machs provided further family clues and directed Tom and Olga back to Prague to visit Olga's father's cousin, Aunt Zdena, then 83 years old.

# Zdena Ješinova Nykličková

*M*y dear Olinko and Tom,

I beg to forgive me, that I am writing so late, but I was a long time ill.

To day I want to express you from the whole heart many thanks for your lovely letter, nice pictures and supplement. You have made us a great pleasure.

I am enclosing the letter for your father. Probably he can say you then more as I in my English.

Please, forgive my mistakes, but I have from the school before 63 years much forgotten.

With a great pleasure we shall to expect the photos of your family and then the visit of you all in the next summer.

I shall tray to writte you after a short time. We send to you all the best wishes and many greetings.

Yours,
Zdena and Francí, with the whole family.

P.S. this is *my first* English letter!

~~~

Prague, 18 November 1996

Dear Vendí,

First of all, please excuse me to Olinka that I'm writing so late. I was sick and am still not all right - I still feel very weak. However, it is a high time to contact you. Thanks to the dictionary, I put together a letter for Olinka and Tom!

Concerning our health, Francí has some trouble with his heart, but it's still quite good. He helps me very much, especially with shopping. I have an arthrosis of right hip, so I cannot walk without a cane. We already had a golden wedding on 26 April 1991!

Between 1949 and 1970, I was employed in a Keramice foreign corporation and achieved the title of "Leading Techno-Economic Reviewer," which helped me to get a good retirement. Francí was working in car repairs in Vršovice until the retirement.

In these days, I am very often thinking of our youth—how I used to run to my aunt in Vysočany for a sour cream sauce, how we grazed a goat in the Balkans, and how you liked being with Auntie

Betynka in Žižkov. This has been a happy time for us – even if in poverty.

Now there is a TV show *We Do Not Give Up Freedom,* and we have recently watched the creation of airwaves and scenes from the life of airmen in England. You cannot imagine what it was like for me to see you getting off a fighter coming back from the action. You were named there, and there was a doggie running to you. The doggie is certainly also sitting by you in a big photo in the book <u>We Died for England</u> which Olinka brought with her. There were also generals Mrázek and Fajtl speaking on this TV show.

What an unfortunate thing that we cannot meet again. We would have so many topics to talk about! The letter, unfortunately, contains only a fraction of what we have to say each other.

Olinka is writing that she and Tom would like to see Prague again next summer, together with their daughters. I'm very sorry I cannot speak English so well, or I could talk to them more. You can tell them more from my today's letter. I will really try to write something back to them. I still remember the pleasant surprise when they contacted us. I hope we will have more time next time.

For today, I finish my letter with the most beautiful greetings and send a kiss.

Yours,
Zdenčí and Francí


P.S. Of course, all of us join the greetings. Watching movies taking place in Los Angeles, I am always thinking of you, how you lived there. It must have been a beautiful city with the mountains in the background, the mountains where you spent your time.

~~~

Prague, January 1998

Hey Mom and Dad,

I know that I've already told you this over the phone, but I'm having an absolutely amazing time here in Prague. Not only do I love the city, the people, and the history, but I also love the arts and the topic we are researching. It's simply fascinating!! ☺ In a country that has so much in terms of art and culture, it's a shame that there is no one to support them. Perhaps people in the States need to learn more about the situation out here—a true art lover would not be able to visit this country without wanting to help fund the conservation and restoration that museums, galleries, and even national monuments need.

This has been a great vacation/work period that will stick with me always! Thank you again for letting me come! I'll talk to you both soon! I love you lots!

Heart,
Catharine (Kati)
XOXO

# Jesus and the Cherry Blossom

*O*n 2011, I met a Japanese amiga partying on a friend's Manhattan rooftop, a rooftop that according to local lore had once belonged to Nick Cannon and Mariah Cary. My new friend sadly had to move home to Japan for visa purposes and sent a farewell email to 50 of her friends, graciously including me, inviting any of us to visit her in Tokyo. Apparently I was the only one who hit reply and typed, "Yes!"

We planned my visit for spring of 2012 when the cherry blossoms would be in fullest bloom. I flew from New York to Los Angeles to meet my love bug of a goddaughter who had just been born and to celebrate Easter Sunday with immediate and extended family. Monday I flew to Tokyo, and what began was a grand adventure starting with pink champagne, specifically Moët at midnight. A trip that could easily have felt *Lost in Translation* flourished into one fit for a dignitary. My Japanese amiga proved the consummate host, not just for Tokyo but for Kyoto and Ise as well.

We meandered along Chidorigafuchi, the cherry tree lane outside her house, nibbled cherry blossom mochi, and sipped cherry blossom-adorned sake. However, one particular event at the start of our adventure stands out. These were the days when the Tsukiji tuna auction was at its inner-Tokyo location and had its renowned tuna auction daily before sunrise. Queues began at 2 a.m. One morning we arrived to find it closed; the next morning we were too late, and the line had met maximum capacity. We wandered the grounds then sneaked past the guard into the wholesale market. What a wonderland! I had never seen anything like it, with larger tuna on the scale of 400 kilos.

One fisherman noticed my marvel at it all and encouraged me to hold his sword while posing for a photo on my camera. The swords are heirlooms passed down from generation to generation. "I've never seen any Tsukiji fisherman give his Maguro sword to tourists to hold—them's are long and sharp! You were very blessed," confided my host. We bought what seemed like $100 worth of toro wholesale for the yen equivalent of $14, picnicked by the Imperial Garden Park's moat under a rising sun, and hashtagged it #breakfastofchampions.

The adventure continued throughout the country along these lines of myriad graces to the extent that post-sojourn, "I am willing to give your God a chance." Thus began a beautiful friendship, soulful and soul-filled.

# Roots and Blooms

*O*n 2017, I stopped running literally and metaphorically. A friend and I flew to Panama for five hours of yoga each day with our teacher in the coastal jungle of Cambutal six hours west of Panama City. Experimenting with science so as to create experience, we stayed salty and played yoga.

At the start of the retreat, the group had an Intention Setting Ceremony–a brilliant idea it seemed, to be mindful of what are one's aims both for the trip and also for life at large upon return. Intriguingly, while in common parlance an intention is a commitment to carrying out actions, in medicine, an intention refers to the healing process of a wound. My intention, in the spirit of Květa, became to bloom where planted.

I came to understand *samadhi*. "*Samadhi* is a beautiful word," explains Osho, a man with whom I disagree fundamentally about Jesus, mathematics, and love though respect deeply for other understandings. "It means now everything is solved. It means *samadhan*, everything is achieved…. You have come home."[13] This connotes the already but not yet of a physical world healed

---

[13] Osho, Yoga: The Science of the Soul (New York, NY: St. Martin's Press, 2002), p. 119.

by supernatural grace. I came to comprehend how memories of our destiny, those memories either actively sought and remembered or eternally whispered and etched upon our souls, can fold time in upon itself in a restorative manner. Therein lies a peace that passes understanding.

Our night flight home to New York City from Panama City arrived before dawn. Swift to get home and unpacked, I fell into a deep sleep at 9 a.m. and woke up at 5 p.m. It so startled me that I picked up a pen and started to journal:

> *It is Monday, 20 March 2017. The water bottle has been drunk, and the sleeping pill remains on the bedside table. I am waking up in Manhattan though feel as though I am waking up into Life. Forty hours ago I was practicing a flow of asanas surfside in Cambutal, beach walking to the sunrise, and re-dedicating my practice, my life, to God our risen Lord.*
>
> *Savasana finally, after decades, happened. If everything dead really has fallen away, I am extremely curious to witness what comes next. There is no hurry. I am waking up. Again.*
>
> *The first time I was 4, and almost 40 years have passed. Still very much in Him, this seems a multi-dimensional rebirth. Maybe it is course correction akin to barnacles falling off a seafaring vessel come into shore.*

*My desires have fallen away. It feels like bliss, it feels like I am stoned, it feels like an awakening to the present. Panama stoned me to stillness. It decommissioned me so that I could be commissioned.*

*I woke up today.*

Following this sojourn in Panama, no one day would ever again feel quite like the next. Rather, each day progressed into a new posture. Life's intentional and experiential mode took on a vinyasa quality wherein the sequence of days interlinked to form continuous flow toward shalom.

Shalom has been described as the modality where everything is right, perfectly woven, interwoven. I felt shalom. It felt more profound than the lack of brokenness and derived from a living dynamic. It brought forth a sense of living and being in the fullest while existing in rich humble rapport.

Sin is the vandalism of shalom, whereas salvation humanizes us. Salvation restores us to make us human again. Accordingly, life stability could be argued to result from a confident view of a capable God. This modality would have three moral imperatives: To cultivate peace in love, strengthening others and eliminating discord; to cultivate joy, independent of the circumstances; and to indulge others' failures with the graciousness of humility. The examined life most certainly can be worth living, and the ripple effects can be infinite.

Even so, I wondered if what we see in part now and one day will see in full would wreck us if we saw it all in full majesty now — such joy, such intimate interconnected and dynamic worship, radiant glory, and exquisite honor. I wondered post-Panama if technology, specifically communication through technology to the exclusion of offline affinities and silent meditations, enabled the numbing of our collective wisdom, the degradation of richness of rapport with God longitudinally and with each other laterally. Could digital culture outstrip humanity? Re-righted with the Almighty, I decided to love people, with presence and with purpose, in the here and now.

Shortly after returning from Panama, I swam through a grief of Implausible Blue with a friend I had met at a wine party for a new local church plant. We embarked upon an adventurous and elegiac journey through Greece, to honor the life and commemorate the loss of his brother 24 years prior off of Lefkada Island in the Ionian Sea. In the manner of pearl formation and with Nancy Drew-style curiosity, Spirit-filled sensitivity, and Homeric temerity, we layered the expedition with beauty and steeped it in history through also exploring Athens' acropolis, Corfu's tranquility, Delphi's oracle, Meteora's James Bond quotient, and Corinth's apostolic love. With much laughter and a few tears, it unfolded as an extraordinary journey that came at tremendous cost of remembrance.

In retrospect, I do not think that either of us knew what to do with Greece and how to process it, at the time. When Heaven is revealed to us, we cannot fully comprehend it. Yet there are glimpses, and I glimpsed it at Delphi's spring visually, with words, colors, shapes, and time sequenced into a moment. I saw that the layering of time could lend freedom for future generations.

# Harlem Honey

"Try our house sangria," the Ponty Bistro bartender beckoned.

"Oh no," I demurred.

"You really want the house sangria—the red one," he championed. "There are two. The red one is the best one."

"Ohhhh," we said.

"Yeeeah, it's got the most booze." We laughed.

"Where are you from?" I inquired.

"Africa," he replied.

"Where in Africa?" I probed.

"Cote d'Ivoire," he provided.

I so very much need to cry, she said more to herself than to me, but there are too many people in my life. It's okay, I shrugged, go ahead and cry. She turned her barstool toward the bright December sun pouring through the French-African bistro window and welled up with weariness. Lamentation at that moment seemed like windshield wipers for life's tears. Swish swish, drip drop, and just maybe finally a ray of sunshine peeks through. It might be a mere mustard seed of sunshine. That little seed can grow into such a mighty tree of 20 feet. Exceptional plants with ideal conditions can reach 30 feet. Imagine! If the world were a perfect art, we would each have our part, each of us an exceptional plant flourishing and fostering ideal conditions for others, for others some of whom might need a seed.

I think I just need to forgive myself and move on, she said. What does that mean, I asked. (I never understood that concept, 'forgiving one's self.' Forgiveness hurts, forgiveness costs, and stealing from Peter to pay Paul never really made sense.) She cocked her head and exhaled. You know what it means? It is something we tell ourselves to prevent collapse into nervous breakdown. You have had quite a bit of burden to bear these past 10 years, I said. She nodded, more to herself than to me.

Do you go to church, I entreated. We used to, she chuckled. We called it Stand Sit Kneel Stand Sit Kneel Repeat. We laughed. Oh yes I agreed, it really can feel like that. Then I added, I sometimes like to sit when people stand. My mom Olga you should see her, she sneaks into church in her Pilates gear with coffee—once even lidless! These tiny protests at rigid ritual effectively enhance the pulsing reality of right relationship. Mmm, she nodded and continued; yes it could be like doing date night differently to keep the love alive minus the arm and a leg for a sitter and dinner. There are other ways to be happy, she added rather glumly.

I don't think the purpose of life is to be happy, I said. Oh? I think the purpose of life is each to optimize our unique set of gifts, and through offering those gifts vertically to God and horizontally to each other even if perseveringly there can be a truly rooted joy. There might even be happiness at points along the way. Yes, she declared, I so very want that! That's my understanding of God, I said. I want to go to a church with sermons like *that*, she pined. Hey, want to come over for an espresso?

"Květa," the bartender mused aloud, after he had processed my credit card to pay for the bill. "It's Czechoslovakian, isn't it?"

"How did you know that?" I marveled.

"I don't know what it means," he smiled.

"It means blossom," I explained.

"Blossoms for honey?" he wondered rhetorically.

We went back to her home and sipped espresso, black, and she told me a story about morning meditations with coffee involving a rather elaborate ritual of frothing a particular brand of almond cashew milk. You have to be very specific it is from such-and-such brand and is this one particular flavor, she admonished; otherwise it is not the same. See, I giggled, you do have religion after all! Would you make me one now, I asked? She beamed.

Now, I between you and me dear reader still like my espresso black, but who at moments such as this one needs to be religious about something like that? She peeled a persimmon, and we sipped these bespoke holy cappuccinos while nibbling the apricot-y fruit, remarking on her current kitchen design, and meandering to remembrances of kitchens past. Did you always live in Harlem, I asked? No my first apartment...oh how I *loved* that little place.

It seemed that we each had lived in a fifth floor walk-up that felt like a haven on a cloud. We daydreamed nostalgically aloud until she came back to the present and exclaimed, hey, that blossom story — do you like honey? She jumped up to grab a jar. Our neighbors have bees, she explained, and the bees here in Harlem make the best honey.

I confess I had not been so surprised in quite a while. Of course bees in Harlem make honey! Suddenly it felt like our very own Blue Zone, Harlem grown.

# Praying Goddaughters

$\mathcal{A}$ winning and memorable Cards Against Humanity round astutely recognized that "Science will never explain <u>my relationship status</u>." My niece who is also my goddaughter was 3 in 2015 when visiting for Christmas in Connecticut. She looked straight at me before tucking into bed one night and asked if I were married. No, I replied, not yet. I was 41 at the time. Snuggling under the covers she squeezed her eyes shut and said a prayer that went something like this: "Dear God, please help Auntie Annie meet a beauuuuuuutiful handsome man very soon so that they can have a beautiful baby girl that I can play with and help take care of. Amen." It was the sweetest boldest most specific prayer.

I kept my eyes wide open after that. A month later through a friend, I met what could fit the bill of a beautiful handsome man. He took me to dinner, I left for Sri Lanka, and he took me to dinner again two weeks later promptly upon my return. His disposition revealed itself to be a bit dull albeit reliable, and I felt ready to welcome dull and reliable and good looking. On our third date he elegantly wondered if I wanted to make a long weekend out of his business trip to Mexico City, and could he pay for my ticket. Dull flew out the window.

Dull boomeranged back in through the same window out of which it flew fairly swiftly. Glass half full-hearted all the same, I came home to Manhattan from Mexico City with a renewed appreciation for mezcal. Having absentmindedly neglected Duty Free, I trotted over to Wine67 on Columbus to buy a bottle. A wine tasting was underway with seven wines set up on a makeshift table directly in front of the liquor shelves. I obliged and did the tasting. Each wine I enjoyed, the girl next to me did not enjoy, and vice versa. By the sixth one I acknowledged her palate and joked that we could be great friends–of the cake versus frosting sort or the crust versus dough sort–with tastes so inversely correlated.

"But I am not really here for the wine. I just want them to move that table so that I can get to the mezcal."

"Mezcal, I love mezcal!"

"I just got home from a long weekend in Mexico City."

"I live up the street here, and my parents live just outside Mexico City!" She passed through Duty Free multiple times a year and got the good stuff. A friendship of complements was born until it ran its course two years later when she moved away.

Meanwhile, the handsome dull man treated me well enough for six months and then said he could not do 'this' anymore and dumped me in a little park in TriBeCa by Spring Place. He did want to honor taking me out for my birthday dinner—at a location once home to Andy Warhol and once the live-in studio of Jean-Michel Basquiat—because the reservation was hard-to-come-by and already on the calendar. He oozed *saudade* and looked so forlorn that my soul both understood and could not understand. We parted with me in tears. My father had also told me that afternoon that he had very serious cancer, and this could very well have been an additional factor in the tears. That night I wept in recognition of kindness and classiness being paired with cowardice.

Two years later at a Christmas Carols and Cocktail party, the concept of which is a cocktail before, during, and after the switching on of Park Avenue's Christmas tree lights with caroling outside the Brick Church, I had come back to the party pub with my wing woman to look for a louche of a guy who had taken me out a few times recently. Instead, I did a double take at a handsome man. Handsome man did the same. It was he! He appeared glowing with elegance; the uptight melancholy from two years prior had vanished. (Later of course the glow would be reattributed to cocktailing on an unusually misty night.) A date

merrily made itself onto the calendar for dinner
and a play a few days hence.

> *Wing Woman: Thanks again for inviting me
> yesterday, that was fun! I hope you are finished
> with that POS you had been looking forward to
> seeing.*
> *Me: LOLOL I am so beyond thankful for you.
> (POS texted me to call him this morning; he's
> definitely a breadcrumber.) So happy you got to
> meet the handsome man. I am excited for dinner
> and a play Friday.*
> *Wing Woman: Perfect. So but for POS being a
> turd you wouldn't get back with handsome man!
> And LOL I got a drink from both your men.*

At dinner and after the play, the formerly
handsome man remained kind, presented a little
less classy, and exuded a dry almost brittle quality
from within. He admonished me not to get
nostalgic for Mexico because while it was nice to
see me, he resolutely still did not want a
relationship. Well then! "Fancy a shag?" I joked.

Two nights later with my wing woman I met the
man who is My Love at a Sunday afternoon house
party. It was one of those just-add-holy-water
relationships that took root on the spot; the host's
sofa provided a wrinkle in time, and we tessered.
His last name means lucky in Italian, and it is fair
to say that I got Lucky at long last. We recognized

Love in each other, and that allowed us —
structurally in the quantum sense — to take those
steps of faith to fall into Forever Love and do the
mostly enjoyable and sometimes gritty work of
loving each other.

For our first date on Tuesday he took me to a
restaurant in the original Bouley space called
Scalini Fedeli (which serendipitously translates to
Steps of Faith). The following Sunday entailed my
favorite lessons and carols service at church and
also turned out to be his birthday. My dance card
was seasonally chock full of dates and holiday
parties. As such, I invited him to church with the
sweetener of treating to lunch after. Guys I had
dated dragged their feet on coming to church with
me, and I wanted to test the waters. To my
astonishment he said yes! The sermon brilliantly
pointed out light warring army angels as part of
the Christmas story. This was our third date. (Our
second date ended up being impromptu the Friday
prior, to a 15th annual Upper East Side party where
to come as my plus-one he either needed to play
my houseguest or play my serious relationship. He
chose the latter naturally, because it was Truth.)

Synchronicity of mirroring each other into infinity
tethered and bolstered the wonder. Our third date
that began at church fell on a marvelously rainy
day. His taxi driver parted the Red Sea to get him
there well ahead of me. (Lo, I would never be late

again.) He loved the sermon, wanted to come again the next week, and found it personally meaningful and uplifting in this season of grace. I was gleefully gobsmacked though tried to keep my cool. Knowing the Lord is pretty magical, the secret sauce to the screenplay of life. To share that had long been *le beau idéal* for romantic relational reality.

His elder son had just returned from semester-in-Rome and would soon be en route back to college so joined us for the birthday lunch, and then My Love and I hopped down to the Lower East Side in search of Champagne and cupcakes to bring to my girlfriend's artsy downtown house party, a holiday-birthday fête.

The fête dazzled with its live jazz band and a hip, mostly new-to-me crowd. That it was our host's birthday as well as My Love's magnified the rainy December warmth and meaning of the day. Suddenly, unbeknownst to My Love, the formerly handsome man walked in the door. I did nearly spit out my Champagne. There truly are no coincidences in life. Imagine works by Hirst and Warhol and a remarkable Mexican artist who could easily be mistaken for Basquiat adorning the walls of this living room. The three of us are coincidentally standing by the Basquiat proxy. It transcended words.

This was the day My Love knew he loved me. The entirety of the day felt like an illustration of String Theory manifested, an experiential glimpse of the Theory of Everything's oscillatory resonance.

*My Love: Annie, so grateful that you and I got off our respective couches and attended Joe's party that day last week. Thank you for being there to allow us to feel the true love that was right there. When that manifested, it blew away all space and time and God said this is it. And here we are.... I will see you tomorrow with love. You are My Person!*

*Formerly Handsome Man: Hi, Annie, kind of strange to run into you in those circumstances. Right out of a Woody Allen movie!*

The morals of the story are that God works in mysterious ways, when God works swiftly he can move deftly, girlfriends are the best, and God listens to the prayers of his sons and daughters. Also, in the spirit of adding more light to the dark places of the world, choose kindness.

*POS: I'd like to see you, but that could be trouble.*
*Me: Good news all around then. I'm off the market!*

Three years after her sweet and bold bedtime prayer, my goddaughter met My Love twice during the Christmas season in Connecticut. "Bye, Uncle!" she exclaimed on second parting. It took me 10 minutes to process what she meant.

# New Years

$\mathcal{P}$arallel with these love life happenings, I was attending an 18-week course in Judaism at a synagogue on Second Avenue. Judeo-Christian in my understanding of history and reality, I had matriculated in the course as a hangover from a spring and summer boyfriend who was Aussie Orthodox by way of London and Tel Aviv. We had consciously decoupled after a coda upon breaking the fast of Yom Kippur a few weeks prior to the course commencing, and it seemed fitting and right for me to matriculate solo.

I am so happy that I did! While my intention was not to tell people about Jesus and proclaim the power of what happened on the cross in class discussions, the contiguity of Hebrew Scriptures with the New Testament lent resounding depth to timeless truths. Halfway through the course is when I met My Love. He was raised Catholic and had been married to a Jewish lady so has sons raised Jewish. Within our first month of meeting, 2018 became 2019 for the Calendar New Year.

I had recently learned that teshuvah, "to return," to return to the land of one's soul, is a concept related to Rosh Hashana which is the Jewish New Year. Rosh Hashanah had come early in 2018, in September. Rosh Hashana sets us up for Yom

Kippur, the Day of Atonement. I had processed
flow and function of these holidays in the manner
of a *je me souviens* for wrongdoings—a looking back
for errors inadvertently made, deliberate misdeeds,
and outright defiance of God. Remembering
people, those whom I had hurt and who had hurt
me, and then seeking reparation with them flowed
right into the eternal marvel of redemption. My
take away: Horizontally repairing community as
opposed to undermining it necessitated a self-
correcting disposition resting thoroughly on God's
grace. We in this manner could mirror a God of
redemption and restoration, thereby tending to tiny
tears in the latticework of the world. Let petals fall
as they may into poultice.

Connecting with the respective journeys we had
been on throughout the year and connecting with
the people we each wanted truly to be is how My
Love and I approached January 1st. That day we
played our hearts' notes, with reverence and
reflection, and it felt like Eternity took root in time.
"Thank you God. Jesus." "Thank you Lord." There
was a new covenant. We flourished.

We also co-hosted a Red Velvet New Year, a sit
down dinner party for nine with White Elephant as
entertainment; attire was sexy chic. On that eve of a
new year, for our three-week anniversary, he
brought a brilliant bouquet of myriad blooms and
multiple types of flowers. The lilies most moved

me, in their ultimate longevity. They flourished for over two weeks and brought to heart Matthew 6:28-29: "And why do you worry about clothes? See how the lilies of the field grow. They do not labor or spin. Yet I tell you that not even Solomon in all his splendor was dressed like one of these." By January 15th the lilies' time had come, though Baby's Breath remained.

"Time to get more soon, Baby! See you tonight," he said.

"In the language of flowers, you My Love are a perennial," I replied.

"I love you Baby! You are My Perennial," he affirmed, mirroring to infinity.

# An Experiment in Love

We start and center our week going to church for soul nourishment and worship, and we hold court as a team. Remembering our destiny, he reminded me of Psalm 90:12: "Teach us to number our days aright, so that we may gain a heart of wisdom."

"Your Mom, Baby, she recognizes Harmony. Us," he pronounced with wonder and gratitude.

"I love you! I love him too!" Mom did say on the phone the next day.

"I feel soul-rest," he observed that night.

Animated weeknights melted into a relaxed cadence of weekends as lovely as the cadence of breathing, which as my Japanese amiga pointed out is as important to life as love and great wine.

"With the olive and wheat, vines make the ancient trinity.... Life is possible from these," pens Frances Mayes in <u>A Year in the World</u>. Wine writer Ilka Sirén notes, "It's all about character.... Good wines are boring, and great wines are never perfect. Not in my book at least. What makes a great wine truly great is the x-factor, that certain edge that will make you howl like a wolf to a full moon. Great wines are not necessarily easy or even very tasty at first. In fact they can be downright nasty. But when they reach that perfect moment and release all their potential, it's magical."

My Love is a beautiful handsome [brilliant, gorgeous, flawed like the rest of us] man, 50% Italian with blends of Alsatian-French and Hungarian. We began with indulgences of Italian quintessence, although a dinner at Balthazar, brunch at Bar Boulud, lunch at La Goulue, film at FI:AF, and nibble of smuggled Alsatian *foie gras* swiftly reminded us of how much more the world has to offer. God took us on an astonishing loop dee-doo, through temples, bars, churches, clubs, lodges, parks, and streets. Kisses, patience, shortcomings, and grace have bundled into sublimely rooted and rich rapport.

To blossom in Italian is *fiorire*. It connotes laughter and involves efflorescing. On one of those early winter nights, after we had made a meal and repaired to read, I lay supine on the sofa while he kicked out the footrest and nestled into a beige leather La-Z-Boy that was Vendí's, my Grandpa Václav Hájek's, through his final years. I had bought all my other furniture to match that old La-Z-Boy. Life had flourished such that it finally fit.

# Praying Mothers

$\mathcal{T}$he Battle of Dunkirk in France was May through June of 1940. Soon thereafter, France capitulated to the Germans who then started bombing England, and that led to the Battle of Britain. The Czech pilots had been flying for the French, but when the French capitulated, the Czech pilots went to Britain. Initially they flew Hurricanes in the air war but soon were flying Spitfires as production of the latter increased. Initially the Czech flyers were mixed into the overall air service, but as time went on they formed three separate squadrons — one bomber squadron and two Spitfire fighter plane squadrons. Václav was in CZ Squadron 313. While the very intense Battle of Britain took place in the second half of 1940, the air war with Germany would last until 1945.

During this time, Václav Hájek was shot down once but survived. His plane had sputtered up and down and up and down and finally crashed-landed on a beach in Dover. Years later he matter-of-factly told his daughter, my mom, that he attributed survival to *his* mother's prayers. "He believed in God," my mom tells me, succinctly and resolutely. "He was a hero," she adds. "My dad did not think highly of church, however. He thought it a place where people dressed up for other people and a place that had very little to do with God. My mom would go, though, when there was no service in session. She would sit in the pews and pray while I colored with crayons at the back." It is curious what we remember.

My mom is a patient praying lady. In December 2017, Mom shared a reflection that hit home in my heart: "Through a confluence of events, be ready for a fairy tale ending." I wrote it down. I had become so versed in processing romantic pain that I risked quelling the joy of prospective love.

Later, in 2018, she added, "God is God of all time. That means prayer can be retroactive, so He can act *in* time." I wrote that down, too. This God outside of time entering time resonated richly with returning, remembering, and repairing.

Later, in early 2019, she continued, "When I was at the pool today, I felt the deepest pangs of love for your Love." I wondered then if a retroactive restitching were underway, a redemptive soul stitching and restoration of this life's latticework for fullest flourishing.

# The Symbiosis of Life and Art

*When you look at the world, what is it that you see? People find all kinds of things that bring them to their knees.* These U2 lyrics were on my iPod in September 2009 for a run around Hanoi's Lake of the Lost Sword. I had arrived in Vietnam just before midnight the day prior and woken early to go for a run before meeting a duo of photographers with whom I would apprentice for the next couple weeks. I paper-napkin-math calculated that three Hanoi lake loops would approximate one Central Park reservoir run. After my first loop along an outer paved perimeter, the number of locals up early doing what appeared to be Tai Chi along that perimeter prompted me for the second loop to hug the rocky willow-lined path closer to the lake. I glanced down to change my music and ducked beneath the willow branches when thwack! It felt like finding the lost sword smack in the head. A thick tree branch hidden by wispy willows had clocked me.

I lost vision that first day in Hanoi during this morning run along that Lake of the Lost Sword. Our world flashed white, gray, black, brightly highlighted shapes, and gray dotted fuzz. It then presented as a memory of shape and color. We are so intricately woven! A Vietnamese man—presumably one of the many doing waterfront Tai

Chi—proved an answer to prayer for this weaving, wandering, and wondering-what-to-do-now traveler. He led me by the hand to a bench, sat me down, and swiftly commenced pressure point head massage. Others joined him, spontaneously and generously rubbing what smelled like Tiger Balm between my fingers. One woman spoke French; I explained being *aveugle*. The sundry crew kept massaging deliberately and without hurry. Sight eventually flashed in, out, and back finally steadily; the woman hailed a taxi, dropped me at my inn, and would not accept so much as even fare for reimbursement. Likely she and he were young adults during the American War. Eternal thanks continue to this day for that man and that lady.

Kindness without motives: May it be a model. Thus began the journey of apprenticeship to a professional photographer and award-winning Canadian film producer who spearheaded the trip with her author-photographer cousin to work with NGOs and visit local tribes. Talk about learning to shoot from a different lens!

My former pastor prior to this trip had regaled a story of when he more fully fathomed God's magnitude, glory, power, and mercy. He had been a seminary student when a teacher compared the distance between the earth and the sun as that of a sheet of paper's thickness. The distance between the earth and the nearest star would be a stack of paper 70 feet high. The diameter of a galaxy would be a stack of paper 310 miles high, and that galaxy is a mere speck in the universe. Jesus Christ the Creator God made the universe and holds it together by the power of His word. Is this the kind of person you ask into your life just to be your assistant?[14] No, you make him Lord.

The implications of this illustration and its reflective question that morning in Hanoi struck me more mightily than the branch. A heartfelt prayer of deepest need poured succinctly and sincerely from my heart: "Jesus, please help." I do not know what I would have done if I had gone blind in Central Park where most people spoke English let alone what I would do in a foreign land with foreign tongues, in a land where the U.S.A. once waged war. We are so wonderfully, fragilely made. Provisional acceptance can be a precursor to experiential understanding. God's intimate omnipotence was definitely displayed in my heart that morning.

---

[14] Dr. Timothy Keller shared this one morning with Redeemer Presbyterian Church in New York City.

# Love in Times of Hormesis

$\mathcal{H}$ormesis is a biological concept describing how through acute stress, a new sort of strength can emerge. Grapes from the old vines, for example, lead to more flavorful wines. When there is mitochondrial dysfunction, cell danger defense modes shift metabolic processes. A cell exists due to how it exists within a network of cells, and that network connects with something outside of any given cell itself. Often in times of medical malaise, our cell danger defense mode can shift metabolic processes making us worse for the wear.

Layering upon this, epigenetics is the study of understanding how we are born from over, outside of, and above our traditional basis of DNA inheritance. Soulfully speaking, then, the whole village can help us or hurt us. Feelings of and from acceptance, compassion, and solidarity — these let health happen.

I realized somewhere along the way that I wanted to be Salt, and I wanted to let Light. A tenacious optimism was emerging, a strength without hardness, a sweet stability that encouraged me to See. By Seeing I could help bring into Being.

"I require deep connection," confided one dear friend. "But do not we all?" I exclaimed.

God has invited us to co-create a renewed world together. It is an invitation to build into the future. This advocacy to re-humanize the world, this is the gospel; God, the ultimate Artist and Creator, is superfluous, extravagant, and abundant inasmuch as we exist. What we do here now matters for Eternity, permanently sketched if we do it in faith. Living and thinking generatively, we can help heal at a mitochondrial level.

Vertical love in the holy sense can put the horizontal plane of loves in proper penultimate light. Winds of freedom thus can blow, and so may our ships sail on the winds of grace.

# Plate Tectonics

"Wherever you are, Love is," he whispered. It was an End that made her want to Begin, yet she lacked words for longtime love. Nordic sunlight cast celestial glow through the fountain's waters.

"Where does love go to die?" she wondered quietly or aloud. Then a marvelous wind remembered deference to the heart and aliveness to the soul. The earth shook, the gales blew, and the birds still sang above the leaves' loud rustle. Mirth emerged, and what was burden became blessing.

# William Arthur

*O*ne day she boarded NJ TRANSIT at New York City's Penn Station to get to Newark in order to catch a flight to Los Angeles for friend and family reunion. The train sat in the station for 40 minutes, at which point in a moment of panic she jumped off, dashed to the street, and hailed a cab. There were no moments to spare, and she shared this with the driver. To this day she still does not know how she made that flight. Traffic gridlocked into the tunnel then suddenly parted like the Red Sea; a man had whisked and waved them through it.

Before hopping out at Newark's departures curb, she glanced at the driver's registration and noticed the name. "Thank you, William Arthur." She made the flight by seconds and said a prayer of thanksgiving for William Arthur.

William Arthur exhaled. He smiled and re-entered New York City, oddly encouraged by hormetic events of the day.

# Praying Fathers

When I was well over 40, my dad wrote a short piece about an answer to prayer for the 5-year-old me. I had never known his vantage let alone the details.

## A Wonderful Answer to Prayer

On Wednesday, 4 June 1980, I was in Jakarta, Indonesia on business, and in the middle of the night I received an urgent call from my office to call home. Our oldest daughter Anne, age 5, had been walking her bicycle through the crosswalk at Royle School earlier that day and had been hit by a truck due to an inattentive driver. She had been thrown about 18 feet and was lying unconscious in the middle of Mansfield Avenue. Anne was rushed to the emergency room at Stamford Hospital and then moved to Greenwich Hospital for neurological care. She remained unconscious with a severely fractured skull through Saturday afternoon when she briefly awoke, but she then relapsed into further unconsciousness.

I made flight arrangements to return home as soon as possible with the help of some truly understanding airline personnel, and my long, very worrisome, sleepless, and prayer-filled flight took me through Singapore, Tokyo, and then on to New

York. I arrived at JFK mid-morning on Sunday, 8 June and then came directly to the Greenwich Hospital where I found Olga in prayerful vigilance with close friends and some medical attendants. Anne still remained unconscious, and due to a number of her issues, including a large and growing hematoma, they were anticipating surgery later that day. After several minutes of update and continued prayers, one of the nurses suggested that everyone except me leave Anne's room, and that I remain alone with Anne. I sat alongside Anne's bed, spoke softly to her, and entered into the most heartfelt prayer that I could ever imagine.

After about 20 minutes, and to my absolute amazement and tearful relief, Anne then awoke from her unconscious state. I called Olga into the room, and we were suddenly hugely hopeful and utterly thankful. The doctors were appropriately cautious and ordered continued rest and quiet for Anne, but very soon after she regained consciousness, we were able to speak coherently with her. Anne never relapsed into her days-long unconscious state, she never had to undergo any surgery, and her further recovery was quite rapid and complete.

Olga and I have continued to offer prayers of thanksgiving for this miraculous and unforgettable recovery of our daughter. It was without question one of the most significant answers to prayer that we have encountered, and this experience has totally and unequivocally reaffirmed our Christian faith.

~Tom Haack, 29 April 2017

# To Write: How, What, When, Why, and For Whom

"For a hypothetically supersensitive being, there would be no 'flowing' of time. The universe would be a single block of past, present, and future," notes Carlo Rovelli in <u>Seven Brief Lessons on Physics</u>. I finally began in late 2018 at the age of 44 to write a memoir traversing time, person, and place. It became a meditation.[15]

In 2017, during an impromptu side trip from Venice to Verona, I spent the night at an inn around the corner from Juliet's fabled balcony and up the street from Romeo's residence. The inn bordered a square and could be reached by cobblestone walkway that wound beneath an arch. A shuttered green wooden window that was nestled in the old stone above the arch mesmerized me. I stopped in the shadow of the stone and gazed up. Then the spell broke, and I advanced into the light of the piazza. At that precise moment of stepping forward, a pigeon fluttered, and a feathered quill floated down into my hand. This is a true story.

---

[15] My yoga teacher explains, "'To meditate' does not only mean to examine, observe, reflect, question, weigh; it also has, in the Sanskrit, a more profound meaning, which is 'to become.'"

"There is no uncertainty in God's ethereal 'post' to you via fair Verona," noted my wise Japanese amiga who at the time was on French holiday drinking in the history of Orléans.

Artist and author Makoto Fujimura in <u>Silence and Beauty</u> perhaps best explains the How to write and When to write: "The timing of my writing seems foreplanned by imperceptible and deliberate divine guidance, and as I write this, I am simply peeling away at my own experience to the core of such providence." With this spiritual exhortation and cosmic encouragement, I came to perceive too For Whom I would write and Why: I began to write for the current and future generations, such that more of us could opt in to better discerning destiny.

# Love, War, and Dating

*H*ow intertwined are love stories and war stories. Most everyone has a love story, and most everyone has a war story. Sometimes those stories are one and the same. In this landscape of life, we can build each other up along the way with kindness, gentleness, merriment, and wisdom shared, or we can tear each other apart with disservice, brutality, misery, and indiscretion. The narrative proceeds accordingly.

It dawned on me upon return from Panama that we are not created just to make this world less horrible, but we are also able to make it more wonderful. As opposed to providing anesthetic, we can cultivate aesthetic. According to the Talmud, "Words from the heart enter the heart." Tony Bennett croons, "With each word your tenderness grows, tearing my fears apart." A mellifluous soul resting in God's grace knows the proverbial peace that passes understanding and sates voracities specifically while filling longings exquisitely. As in Savasana, the detritus and toxins fall away as proper perspective and temperate, delicate proportion get restored.

I vividly recall a particular morning post-Panama at LaGuardia awaiting a delayed pre-dawn flight to Wisconsin for an extended family wedding. I had met my mom and dad at the gate and felt bleary for lack of sleep so curled up like a child on the floor beneath my mom's puffy coat to nap. In that lucid state of sleep, I was aware of a generational spiritual reset at the intercellular level. It produced a radiant rest upon waking and boarding. I was never quite the same again.

"Put me first," is how I have come to understand the first Hebraic commandment. It commands a primary Love. My, oh my, what it takes for each of us truly to understand that He lovingly jealously really means it! It cost him everything. "Acquire your soul with patience," writes Luke (21:19). What goes into the science, art, and practice of being rightly related and fully present in each humdrum moment of every day entails mindfulness, right heartedness, and creative fullness atop an abundance of grace. I wonder if we were intended to multi-task as much as we do.

"Vision imparts moral incentive," observes Oswald Chambers. In other words, focus the heart on what God is doing, and it will realign ideals and appetites. Expect great things from God, notably beyond what I can imagine, and then if He gives me a glimpse, meditatively pray it through. God is a God of abundance — in costly love, majestic splendor, and eternal provision. There is bona fide power, an actual reparative and course-correcting power, in what happened on the cross. Life is not cheap; rather, it is priceless. Love is a choice, and love is a function.

Irrespective of love, these are lessons I have learned, in no particular order, thanks to men I have dated:

- CitiBike makes certain tricky treks in Manhattan a breeze.
- A stone bath mat absorbs water, looks classy in a granite bathroom, and feels good on bare feet.
- The difference between 5 milligrams of cannabis and 15 milligrams of cannabis is a big deal.
- Eat before the party.
- Don't order wine at a dive bar and expect it to be vintage.
- Food shared makes life that much warmer.
- Billecart-Salmon pairs with everything, especially at lunch.
- Foreplay is underrated.
- Order the squash blossoms!
- If he is stealing honey jars from work to gift your mom for Christmas, he might also be cheating on you.
- Staten Island has baseball.
- A French car designed to run on gas will not run well for long after the tank gets filled with diesel in Spain.
- Making out in cabs is fun.

My Japanese amiga once observed that sometimes love is a colored paper heart with sticky tape on one side, blowing clumsily in the wind. Catch it. Pick it up. Carry it tenderly. If stars do not align, and if hearts do not align, the God who created the universe, the stars, and the hearts can most certainly do something about that. Take rest in such knowledge, rest at the mitochondrial level. A patient and waiting heart may find breath here.

# For Love to Last

"How did you understand who I was and who I wasn't?" This thought bubbled up from my subconscious one morning.

It was uncanny how of the 88 countries to which I had mentioned traveling, he asked if I had yet been to Poland. I had returned last month. I asked if he ever came to the city, and he said all the time. I asked if he wanted to be my guest for a Juilliard recital, and he said he would love to join me, had always wanted to see the inside of the school. He asked if he could take me to dinner after and found my favorite secret sushi spot and wondered if it would be acceptable. I exclaimed how his Spidey Sense was delightful, and he blushed that his inner Marvel child was now satisfied. Afterward he called to make sure I got home safely. He thanked me for the wonderful night. He asked to see me again, via text. I called and said no, not romantically like that. He texted that I was a tremendously wonderful and classy person, that he is so happy to have spent one evening with me, that he is sad about it, that he is thankful for the recital, and to take care.

He was so in tune that he scared me a bit. I realized in an instant that men could expertly plan dates and deftly build anticipation with consecutive dates. I realized that as ladies and gentlemen treating each other as ladies and gentleman, people could put one another honorably and insightfully at ease. I wanted a relationship like that but greater, a sequence of dates not just with any same person but rather specifically with My Person — my person with whom to experience what J.R.R. Tolkien describes as "joy beyond the walls of this world," a romantic love and deep friendship that touches on eternity. I realized I had already met My Person. Two people connected through heavenly intelligence, bowed with reverence, and treasured in esteem: This is what I for so long had wanted, and in that instant I realized who was My Love.

# A Doorway to Adventure

We have heard the aphorisms on friendship. "To have a friend, be a friend." "Make new friends, but keep the old; one is silver and the other gold." The way people in the 1960s remember where they were when Neil Armstrong first stepped on the moon or when JFK got shot, I remember vividly when I made a couple of what are at-a-glance the unlikeliest of friendships.

Having just returned home to Manhattan from an Ilyrian-Dalmatian-Istrian coastal exploration inclusive of Albania, Montenegro, Bosnia Herzegovina, Slovenia, and Croatia in autumn of 2014, I attended a Zankel Hall performance where Brooklyn Rider performed six different composers' pieces. The final composer was in the audience. The quartet introduced him as an Albanian cellist who had studied at Juilliard. I was so surprised at the coincidence and confluence that at the after-party up on the terrace, I met the cellist and exclaimed how I returned only yesterday from a trip involving Albania and lived by Juilliard. Well the surprise proved mutual. We worked with each other for a spell after that, me helping him better convey his story and expertise on his website. He paid me in music, artistic angst, and red wine.

One night the cellist composer's score for a short film debuted at the Players Club on Gramercy Park. We went, and at drinks beforehand I met a man playing pool with a quirky glove on one hand.

"What's that?"

"That? That's my bionic thumb." In New York, anything is possible. "I'm a stuntman." It made sense, being that we were at a private social club for the theater community. Later he caught me and conceded, "It's not a bionic thumb. It's a pool glove. But I am a stuntman. You were so sweet about the thumb, please allow me properly to introduce myself. I'm David."

Four years later David and I had an Aristotelian friendship: "Wishing to be friends is quick work, but friendship is a slow ripening fruit." He had come to my parties as I had gone to his readings; we would sip bourbon at the Players or enjoy happy hour at Maialino and talk about life. He always had larger than life stories too, the 'hit me harder' one with Robert DeNiro in Raging Bull being my favorite. He loved training his former stunt horses Dusty Darling and Cinbad, was at peace with his ex-wife, devoured books, and worked as a trainer to creative legends in film and music. He was a thoughtful guy.

One day as thanks for a drink, I left a gift-wrapped copy of C.S. Lewis' <u>Mere Christianity</u> for him at the Players because it resonated with practical themes and history that threaded our discourse. (I once gifted this book, in the spirit of 'please understand me,' to a boyfriend who threw it unopened into the trash. A tiny bit of scar tissue from that admittedly lingered for a spell.)

"Our holiday reservation is set at Novitá, on Monday, at 6:30 p.m. Once again, thank you for the thoughtful gift. It is nice to read a morally uplifting book during these times."

"Beautiful, thank you, I am so very much looking forward. And you are welcome. It is a Christmas and Chanukah theme, that of adding more light to a dark world. There is so much to celebrate."

After an afternoon of sunshine and teatime with a girlfriend in Brooklyn and a dip into the Karl Lagerfeld treasure trove at Neiman's so as to emerge newly dressed and shoed, I met David for a bottle of red and tasting menu of shared plates.

He lately loved WWII books though felt the angst of the darkness, death, destruction, and double-crossing in the storylines. I joked that this need for literary palate-cleansers is why Chick Lit exists as a category.

"What book needs still to be written?" I asked more seriously. He confirmed what I already knew, that there is nothing new under the sun that has not been experienced or written.

"Maybe then it is a matter of remembering?" I mused.

"There are three themes that timelessly resonate," he pointed out, "those that recognize universal aspirations, describe a doorway to adventure, and regale an experiment in love."

The next morning I woke up and wrote.

# Beyond Rangoon

$\mathcal{O}$n tenth grade I lived in northern Thailand with AFS for a summer. AFS France only had a study program, and as a high-stress student during the academic year I had no desire for superfluous summertime stress. Belgium had the home stay with no study program that I sought, but as a French student, I wondered if a summer of Flemish immersion would ruin my accent. My dad then suggested thinking geographically out of the box—China, Thailand, Malaysia. Thailand won.

It worked out swimmingly. I went to school in order to hang out with the English Department, enjoyed the Thai kids' French classes, and learned dancing, cooking, cross-stitching, and basket weaving. The freedom of it not 'counting' for my GPA lent a permission to learn more naturally, and by summer's end along with being able to eat food *ped, makh ma* ("hot, very very hot"), I could hold a conversation in Thai at the market.

My host family lived in Chiang Mai, and I had three little sisters. Our grandmother, Khun Yai, owned a resort up in Chiang Rai, by the Golden Triangle. The Golden Triangle had something to do with the drug trade, I learned. I found this fascinating because I had naively thought that I could smoke weed that summer, due to being inactive from Post 53 the volunteer ambulance service on which I served and where we were routinely drug-tested, only to learn that the penalty for drugs in Thailand ranged anywhere from prison to death. It put a bit of the fear of God in me and quelled my interest in drugs during that teenage phase of wanting to experiment with everything. Curiosity could be more fruitfully funneled.

My Thai family and I went up to our Khun Yai's resort one weekend. I remember us driving along a sunny muddy golden river and having a verdant Laos pointed out to me on its other side. We drove along a bit further and came to a military checkpoint for Burma. I really wanted to go to Burma though was not allowed because of 'paperwork,' they told us at the border. That was the summer of my sweet sixteen.

Flash forward 27 years. I watched the movie *Beyond Rangoon* and was moved to tears at the naiveté with which I had so impertinently wanted to enter Burma in 1990. People then were literally dying to get *out* of Burma and into Thailand due to the political situation at the time. Similar to how Ceylon was now Sri Lanka, Siam was now Thailand, and French Indochina was now Vietnam, Burma was now Myanmar. It seemed like the time to go to Myanmar, so I went, flying in and out by way of an overnight connection in Thailand.

Two bookend worthy reunions in Bangkok thus graced the adventure. On the front end, Brandon, another American AFS student from the summer of 1990 who had helped me celebrate my sweet sixteen in Chiang Mai with hard-to-come-by gifts of Hershey's chocolate and Jiffy's peanut butter, happened to be in Bangkok on business February 14th the night I arrived. On the tail end, Nida, the eldest of my Thai sisters, popped down from Chiang Mai. She filled me in on the family and how the house we used to live in had been sold and was now a discotheque. She brought a gorgeous glazed blossom necklace as a gift from a Chiang Mai orchid and flower farm and played the consummate host.

# Exploring Ends of the Earth

 $\mathcal{T}$ agging along with an international crew from the World Bank and Columbia Business School at the start then dovetailing solo from there, in early 2018 I deep dove into the southern hemisphere for three weeks on an exploration of the Chilean longitudinal and latitudinal ends of the earth: Patagonia's glaciers, gauchos, fjords, and penguins from Torres del Paine to Tierra del Fuego; Magellan's Strait; Cape Horn's rocky promontory overlooking Drake's Passage; Santiago's wine country; Valparaiso's colored hills and harbor.

In the tropical Polynesian spirit of 'when in Rome,' this meant also reverently hopping west seven hours to hang out with the moai and soak in Rapa Nui's (a.k.a. Easter Island's) tranquility for a spell during [orthodox] Easter. From icy seas to balmy isles, each day commenced with an hour of twilight yoga beneath the ever present Southern Cross and its surrounding starry skies. The whole and its particulars left me awestruck and overwhelmingly filled with gratitude.

One pair of particulars involves two black-necked swans. They were floating elegantly together on a Patagonian pond's azure waters. It hit me then. Could recognizing real Love be like gazing upon these swans? You knew it when you saw it and often from afar?

My French host-mother during Stanford-in-Paris in 1994 had told me a swan story when I arrived post-EuroRail travels before school began. I had gifted her one of two tiny porcelain swans from the gift shop at Neuschwanstein Castle. Most swans mate for life, she imparted. A mother of two grown girls, she herself had been resplendently married and recently widowed only two years prior. I remember wanting that, wanting to be part of something yet not just anything, wanting no Pyrrhic victories in this arena. My heart understood something timeless at that moment. It felt like spiritual compression, a modality where our hearts can comprehend eternity in warp-time.

Core truths can get tarnished with time. "A little bread and sip of wine, and I'm fine," she murmured, years later, still waiting for the feast. It takes courage and remembrance to keep the cup.

# Walking Warsaw

$\mathcal{I}$ had always wanted to honeymoon in Greece thus never went in the spirit of saving it. Then one spring day in 2009 I woke up and realized I could fly solo so booked a September sojourn that began in Athens. A fellow solo sojourner, whom I had begun to recognize through our similar island-hopping modalities, introduced herself on the boardwalk of Santorini's black sand beach where I was feasting on grilled calamari, and in the spirit of breaking bread together, we shared a carafe. Thus was born a travel buddy for life. She was from Poland and lived in Philly.

Nine years later she invited me to visit her during a month's stay in Poland. I had never been to the country, save for once stepping a foot across the invisible technical border while on a hike in the northern Czech Republic. A life lesson-learned is that when a friend invites me to his or her homeland, a land that is foreign to me, I do not just say yes; I exclaim yes. We AirBnBed it in the New-Old Town—'New-Old' because everything got destroyed in WWII, which meant the Old Town of Stare Miasto got rebuilt after the war. (Warsaw tragically earned the nickname City of Ruin due to the destruction's extent.)

Reading Leon Uris' <u>Mila 18</u> on this trip broke my heart. It viscerally drove home to me how war entails trauma, trauma reverberates often imperceptibly through generations, and how staggeringly recent the war was in terms of generational resonance.

Toward the last day of my stay, in sleep I dreamed what seemed a hallucinatory vision of language. At the moment upon waking, it brought William Blake to heart and mind. I have no idea who is Eloise — my mother, my host, any emigrant returning to a homeland post-exile whether self-imposed or compulsory, or an alternate version of my self. I scribbled it down. The dream-vision went like this:

> *Eloise emigrated, assimilated, and knew a vivid spectrum of the world. She had moved 18 times by the time she was 10. Homemade rabbit pâté (a grandmother's recipe), Côtes du Rhône, and remembrance. The glowing hearth of what was war torn.*
>
> *Eloise wondered, when the day dawned, what were all the possibilities. She blinked at the red dawn, refilled a water glass, and went back to bed, to bed and into contemplation's deep dive. How was it that the golden hours were those that so supremely plumbed depths, skipped across waves, talked to God, said Thank You, I Love You, and Help Me?*

The integration of past with present struck me as imperative. What this vision hearkened was a deep empathy for going back: It could be an unspoken going back, a physical return, a narrated return, or numerous other permutations of seeing, sensing, lauding, and lamenting. Life is sweeter with a friend. Through going back we can go forward more wholly and felicitously and repairingly.

Fast forward to the 21st century. Olga felt blessed with a lifetime of rich albeit inconsistent experiences and concomitantly recognized that she had been able to bless her children with consistency. She blessed her children with parents who persevered victoriously together, tending to the rose garden outside and lighting the hearth inside the same home for over 40 years. She blessed her children with head and heart knowledge of an unchanging almighty loving God. Her petals became our poultice.

# Home

$\mathcal{H}$aving explored almost the whole wide world, I decided to live locally where I was planted. Let us get back to the business of making merry right here in the concrete jungle of Manhattan, this Athens of the modern world. Let us reservoir walk. Let me host. Let you host. Let us play wing. Lament together, learn together, pray together, praise together. Laugh together. Stop to smell the cherry blossoms. Inhale. Exhale. Look. Listen. Taste. Hear. Feel. Remember at least in part, so that we may become in full.

"Who are the most humble people you meet?" I asked.

"Those who know the most," he replied.

"Late bloomers can make the most beautiful flowers," she observed.

# Beautiful Downtown Burbank

On 2019, Olga received an email from a Burbank high school friend of hers in the 1960s. The name was familiar, but she could not recall a face to match it.

"Let me see if I can refresh your memory," came the reply. "I was the tennis-playing kid with red hair who used to play doubles with you and Judy Seydoux. (I was so saddened to hear Judy passed away a few years ago.) I would pick you up at your apartment to go play tennis and remember meeting your dad and actually was always fascinated by his story…. I was at Cal and came over to visit you when you were at Stanford. Once during a holiday break from school when we were both home in Burbank I took you out to see *Hair* in Hollywood. We had a real date I guess. One of my best friends from Berkeley was in the cast. I thought it was amazing; you were quite horrified by it as I recall! Last time we saw each other was the summer of 1969, I believe, when you were working for Stanford's summer camp at Lake Tahoe. I came up there to visit you."

Olga began to remember. "My dear husband and I have been married for 48 years," she replied. "Getting old has its challenges but is really a lot of fun. And as for memories, it is always great to reflect on our friends and experiences from when we were young. I was just thinking...you have lived a marvelous connected sort of life, whereas I have not. I went to about 20 different schools by the time I was 10 years old! Old memories were just that, never being brought up in the present, for I was busy making brand new friends. No wonder you have no problem bringing up the past, for you could always dip in with a concurrent friend!! At least, as my father always taught me, I learned how to make new friends quickly! My father always said to move on. Writing became impossible because he would always warn me not to say on paper that which I wouldn't want the whole world to know. I had loved writing voluminously, but that put an end to it! So I had no occasion to go fishing for old memories. That's why writing to you of so long ago is such a stirring occasion for me, flexing old muscles I didn't know I had. Do you catch my drift? Literally!"

"Yes," she continued, "you are correct that Tom and I met at Stanford in 1970. Tom was in the Business School, and we were married in 1971 before he graduated. Our first move was to New York City where Tom worked at Merrill Lynch in investment banking. Our first daughter Anne was born in 1974 just as Tom changed jobs and began work at Lazard in midtown Manhattan. We also then moved to Darien, Connecticut. Interestingly, we are still living in our first house (although nicely renovated) and Tom is still affiliated with Lazard (having worked in investment banking as an associate, general partner, managing director, and now a director of the private Lazard company). Our second daughter Catharine was born in 1978. Like you, we have had some wonderful international work experiences including stints in Turkey, China, Indonesia, and Europe. This should be Tom's final year with Lazard, and we are considering moving to some domicile with less burdensome tax policies than Connecticut currently imposes. But we really don't have any place in mind that truly interests us. Anne graduated from Stanford and Harvard Business School and then worked for two tech companies that went public, so she has done well and is semi-retired. She now lives in New York City where her brainy guy friend works in derivatives. Kati graduated from Williams College and moved to Los Angeles after working at Sotheby's in New York City in modern art. She went on to work as a curator and dealer in modern art before getting married and having two fine kids, a boy Trey age 9 and a girl Hutton age 6. They are the highlight of my life, and being a grandparent is wonderful. Kati and her family now live in Manhattan Beach, California. So that is a quick summary of what has been going on in my life for almost a half century. I am very thankful and feel blessed."

Through this discourse, her dicey memories began to flow forth more fluidly: "I do not remember the exact age I stopped my TV/Hollywood life, when my dad pulled me out to avoid a 'casting couch' situation, but it was just before I became a teenager. You might remember a commercial for 'Kix, Trix, and Sugar Jets' where a little girl is taking a little boy by the hand and walking down a path pulling a little red wagon. As they pass a tree they have a conversation with the resident Moon Bird in a series called *Adventures in Cereal Land*. I believe he was the Sugar Jets icon. Then there was another commercial for Carnation Milk, live on an Art Linkletter show when I poured the chocolate sauce on the wrong side of the camera. He wasn't too kind…but it got a laugh."

Memories brought forth more memories: "*Playhouse 90* was the biggest role in my life. It was a series of 90-minute episodes. My episode was called *The Iron Bedstead*. I played an opera star when she was a child who grew up in an abusive home where the parents were fighting terribly on and around the sofa downstairs. It was dark. I was upstairs and ran out on my balcony to sing *One Fine Day*, the Puccini aria from <u>Madame Butterfly</u>:

> *Weeping? And why? And why?*
> *Ah 'tis faith you are lacking*
> *Hear me*
> *One fine day we'll notice*

*A thread of smoke arising on the sea*
*In the far horizon*
*And then the ship appearing*
*Then the trim white vessel*
*Glides into the harbor*
*Thunders forth her cannon*
*See you? Now he is coming*
*I do not go to meet him not I*
*I stay upon the brow of the hillock*
*And wait there*
*And wait for a long time*
*But never weary of the long waiting*
*From out the crowded city*
*There is coming a man*
*A little speck in the distance*
*Climbing the hillock*
*Can you guess who it is?*
*And when he's reached the summit*
*Can you guess what he'll say?*
*He will call, 'Butterfly' from the distance*
*I, without answering*
*Hold myself quietly concealed*
*A bit to tease him and a bit*
*So as not to die at our first meeting*
*And then, a little troubled*
*He will call, he will call*
*'Dear Baby wife of mine,*
*Dear little orange blossom'*
*The names he used to call me when he came here*
*This will all come to pass as I tell you*
*Banish your idle fears*

*For he will return.*[16]

Then I was also on either *Little House on the Prairie* or *The Real McCoys*. I don't think it was *Little House* because I'd have remembered Luke. Anyway, there was a Sunday school class, and I was in that scene. I believe the Mouseketeers had just begun when I came on the scene, and I departed a short time later. I used to take ballet lessons and tap lessons, and my voice teacher said that I had a three-octave range as a kid. But that would have been a huge time commitment…and who knows if then I still could have gotten into Stanford? After Stanford came a short stint at <u>Gourmet</u> magazine and also at <u>Architectural Digest</u>. Then I found the Lord, and it was mainly hosting or attending Bible Studies and raising two wonderful daughters!!"

---

[16]https://lyricsplayground.com/alpha/songs/o/onefin edaydeannadurbin.html

# Laughing with the Moon

*T*he moon rose so swiftly above the clouds. It riveted attentions then dissolved into weed-worthy giggles.

"Please find me," she said, hours later, moments prior to the moon passing directly behind the earth and completely into its shadow. He had been tarrying and not noticed.

"I love you!" he affirmed, subsequent to finding her. It was a total lunar eclipse. "It just took a while for my head to catch up with my heart," he realized.

The Blood Moon became a resplendently bright and full one on a 12 degree Fahrenheit night. In a world of no coincidences, in a shop of myriad bottles, Ben at Wine67 had recommended to them a Portuguese red that bore a wooden netsuke-style ladybug emblem. (As palates had changed, Old World vines replaced New World wines.) They flicked off the red and black wooden ornament, uncorked the Serradinha, and sipped the sacrament beneath the full moon.

They contemplated the little ladybug's wonderful work of soul-stitching marvel and drank in a deep-seated peace. She sensed God restoring each of us to Him and to each other. She sensed the latticework in the created universe. In that moonlit moment they got a glimmer as to how we can each have a part toward restoring the intended design.

# Temerity Toward Tangible Dreams

*T*homas More juxtaposes the ease with which one can speak of morality with the challenge one faces in perseveringly pursuing that design: "You see, we speak of being anchored in our principles. But if the weather turns nasty you up with an anchor and let it down where there's less wind, and the fishing's better. And 'Look,' we say, 'look, I'm anchored…to my principles.'"[17]

"I'm dreaming," he says to her.

"Yes, you are," she replies. "But you must wake."

"I don't want to wake."

"But you must."[18]

Nietzsche notes how "only that which never ceases hurting remains in the memory." The perpetual choosing to continue despite fear or pain defines perseverance, one of the fruits of which is courage. *Braveheart* depicts enduring moral leadership that commoner William Wallace exercised through chosen suffering and accepted responsibility.

---

[17] Robert Bolt, <u>A Man for All Seasons</u> (New York, NY: Random House, 1962), p.69.
[18] Quoted from the movie *Braveheart* (1995).

Wallace perseveringly pursued an objective standard irrespective of convenience. In this manner, he effectively transformed a fragmented 14th century Scottish society from one of suffocating dominion to one of brave, united freedom.

I have not yet been to Scotland. The late Anthony Bourdain put it on my list in his pre-Kitchen Confidential days when he waxed rhapsodic about haggis. I suspect the rite of haggis and Scotch for me will be a sacrament of sorts.

# Fishing

Angling, waiting; nibbling, biting;
Pulling, slackening, tautening, fighting;
Jumping, twisting, glistening, splashing,
Thrashing, gasping, yielding, dying.

"Fishing"
c. 1965, by Olga Marie Hájek

# Facsimile Message

Prague, 23 September 1998

ear Tom and Olga,

Please accept the attached translation as our gift to you both for the many kindnesses you have shown both Kathy and me.

For my part, as you will learn from reading the attached, it was a great honor to translate these memories of your father, Olga. He is truly a great man.

I look forward to translating the copies of other letters that I have.

Best Regards,
Petr Pešek

# Story of the Czech Pilot Václav Hájek

Václav Mach    MEMORIES    Written in 1966

Ohnišov, Czechoslovakia

$\mathcal{O}$n view of the fact that I soon will be 80 and none of us now knows either day or hour,[19] I would like hitherto to summarize the memories and exciting events from the lives of extraordinary men who took my notice. I would like to narrate the destinies and adventures of my son-in-law Václav Hájek. This story is for the memory of members of the family and also as an attachment of the town chronicle, because the future young readers, who did not live through the war, will find in this documentation remembrance of that time and adventure.

For those who do not know the circumstances of how Václav Hájek came here, I have to start from the beginning.

I had a daughter Květa who began going to the foreign language school in Prague to learn English and Russian after the war in 1945. When she

---

[19] Václav Mach's wife, Marie, age 68, passed away 30 October 1965. Born 1 November 1894, he was 71 when he began to write this in 1966.

returned home on the holidays in 1946, she entrusted to us that she had a boyfriend–an officer pilot. Even before she could finish her words, a low flying plane was roaring outside. Frighteningly, she screamed, "Jesus, that is him!" We all ran out, and we saw a plane going in the direction of Janná. The plane turned around and flew back, low over the roofs, leaning to one side. He later said that he recognized my daughter. The plane repeated this unusual theater for us a couple of times. It was for our entire town a sensational event. The plane was a big English plane the "Spitfire." The flight lasted about 16 minutes from Kbely Prague airport to our town. The plane consumed 270 liters of gasoline for the entire flight.

Just for explanation, I would like to add that this boy was a member of the General Staff even during the 1st Republic and, after returning from England, he served at the Ministry of Defense in the air forces department. As an active pilot, he was obliged to engage in a two-hour training flight once per week, to keep himself in good condition.

He had repeated such flight many times when he was in Prague. He already had drawn on the air maps the line that he had to follow to reach Ohnišov. Our town he always recognized by Masaryk's School. His flight was sensational not only for us, but also for the wider neighborhood, in

Bystré, Janov, and particularly in Nové Město where his relatives were on summer holidays.

Today, with certain distance from that time, when the progress in aviation is going so fast, nothing exceptional might be seen in such a thing. Czechoslovakia bought this fabulous aircraft after the war, at a time when the local industry was still in ruins, and those low flights, full of such acrobatic elements, were the event of the day. He came later to the holiday at harvest time by train. At the end of September 1946 was the wedding, and he became a member of our family.

I start slowly and briefly with a narration of his life, based on his explanations and on the explanations of his aunt (who was the sister of his father). She remembers parts of his life he never told us.

His father was the engine driver on the Prague-Budweis (Budějovice) railways, and his father wanted his son to follow him on this job. The son refused, saying that the job was not for him, that this kind of job was boring. The son desired to do something with motors. As a frequenter of the mechanic apprentice school in Strasnice he was in his element. In 1928 when Mr. Masaryk was reelected as president of Czechoslovakia, the factory where he was working gave Mr. Masaryk a luxury car. But shortly after that, the driver returned the car to the factory complaining about

some mysterious breakdown involving a strange
rustle.

It was a big and unpleasant surprise. All the
managers immediately came around, discussing
what happened. And in that moment, one curious
fellow pushed through the crowd of these
managers, because he wanted to see the engine
running from close-up. He placed himself at the
fender, and the strange rustle stopped. He tried
again, to be sure, and, after that, the fellow told his
patron what he had found. The managers,
something of a society of most important men, had
felt humiliated by this young fellow. The
mysterious breakdown and strange rustle was only
a fender that had not been properly fixed to the car.

After going through technical school for four years,
Hájek had to join compulsory army service. He was
serving in a couple of regiments in different places
in the country and also in the armored tank
division. (He called tanks 'moving cremation.') He
went to military academy in Hranice; he passed
through with honors as a flight lieutenant. As a
well-educated, self-made man, he was acting also
as a member of the recruiting board. The recruiting
board conducted the detailed review of all the
applicants for pilots, exploring their abilities and
their conditions such that the years of training and
expense for such men would not be spent in vain.
We were surprised how truly he was able to

determine the nature of people he had never met before.

His parents didn't like his flying. They were scared because the flying seemed dangerous to them. But Hájek did not care, and he was in his element. During the 1st Republic he was serving in an air force regiment in Prague in barracks located at Kbely airport. In pre-wartime, the air forces were growing and maturing. But after 15 March 1939, when Hitler invaded Czechoslovakia, the air force was disbanded. The Kbely airport, its barracks, and its offices were occupied. It was ordered that everything was to stay in place and that the keys to all desks were given to Germans.

The following day, 16 March 1939, the high rank officers from the Czechoslovakian air force's General Staff discovered that important documents and plans remained in one desk drawer. They wanted to remove or destroy these documents, before the Germans found them. There were two sets of reserve keys for the drawer containing these important documents. Hájek had these keys at his disposal. It was a dangerous task, either-or, like in a thriller. One of the two brave soldiers who would risk life to retrieve these documents was Hájek. Certainly they had to have prepared everything, calculated all the risks and possibilities.

They had a governmental car, wore civilian clothing, and hid firearms in their pockets. They drove quickly, without stop, through the German guard at the airport, not stopping until they reached the front door of the office. Hájek quickly hopped out and ran into the office. He rapidly opened the drawer and threw the papers into his briefcase. He closed it and ran back out to the car. As soon as he sat on the car seat, having his leg still on the footboard, the car darted from this place without any control by the German guards. After a couple of minutes of dodging, they found with relief that nobody had pursued them.

They luckily returned back and realized that the task was easier than they expected. It seems that the advantage, which they had, was, in fact, that the Germans at the beginning of the occupation of Prague did not have a clear view about everything, where all the things were. The fast and self-confident movement of the civilian car along with the fact that the car's stopping and Hájek's action did not last more than one minute surprised the German guards. After the German guards recovered from the surprise, and apprised what the care could be, the car was already gone.

Despite the fact that they could have lost their lives on this action, Hájek never narrated this exciting story himself. But as I came to know him, the action was wild, and Hájek would never be the one to sacrifice his life for cheap theatrics. The other fellow was exactly the same king of a guy as Hájek.

Both of Hájek's families were living in Žižkov in one house of flats; his grandfather and grandmother together with his widowed aunt lived on one floor lower than Václav and his parents. That evening on 16 March 1939 Václav stopped by his grandparents and said, "Today I might have lost my life, but everything did fare well." I am repeating only his talk with his aunt. More than that only he himself could clarify.

Thence, early in summer 1939 Hájek escaped together with a couple of his pilot-fellows. They crossed the border to Poland somewhere by Ostrava, and after a couple of days, they reached the Gdynia harbor.

There they were taken on board of a ship with Polish refugees. The ship was sailing the Baltic Sea to the west with an unknown destination. They too desired to fight against the Germans. The journey was very difficult. The Germans already had placed mines in all narrows. The ship was torpedoed but happily escaped. Sailing through certain places only at night, the ship finally reached La Manche channel. All at once the ship engines became silent, and the ship stopped at night. Václav woke up and was listening when, from behind the door, somebody was quietly walking.

He heard knocking on certain cabin doors, and he realized that some people were fleeing the ship by flashlight. Only in the morning did Hájek and his friends learn that about 400 Polish Jews had left the ship, crowded by refugees, and landed secretly in England. The ship further continued through the channel.

The ship was sailing around the coast of France, through the Gibraltar Narrow to the Mediterranean Sea to Toulon's Harbor. And now started the real surprise for all the refugees. The French officials thwarted their plans. Instead of allowing the ship and its passengers free movement and free decision about their further plans and destiny, the French indicated to them that they should decide either to join the Foreign Legion or be sent back to the border of German Reich into the hands of the Gestapo. With bitterness, Hájek and his fellows voted for the lesser evil and recruited themselves to the Foreign Legion and its famous training center in Africa.

Hájek spent three months in this training camp. He went through the hard training. Later he remembered that time as the worst period in his life. In terrible sultry weather they returned from drill squad, exhausted physically and mentally. The ruling authority was strict drill. The sergeant had the right to shoot a soldier who did not follow his command. It was something that was not acceptable for freethinking Czechoslovakian soldiers, and when one day they read in the daily order that the French were looking for pilots, it was immediately obvious what should be their next step. With pleasure they reported to registration so as to be finally out of this hell. Seven Czech pilots sailed on the ship further through the Mediterranean Sea to French Syria to Beirut harbor. There were large oil fields and pipelines leading the oil to the other harbors. Oil is a very important raw material and good in any war, but because the Italian Air Forces often attacked the fields and pipelines, the Allies decided to make anti-aircraft defense of the oil fields stronger.

The military airport was located in the desert, far from the settled coast, but the pilots did not have any problem with the navigation. They oriented themselves by the mountain crest, which they had to 'climb over' after every take off. There were 150 members on staff. One fourth were pilots and the rest technical support and guards. They lived in big camouflaged tents, and the entire camp was surrounded by a barbed wire barrier and was under the permanent protection of guards. The pilots' main service task was to look out over the Mediterranean Sea. It was nothing pleasant because it was so boring for them. The infinite surfaces of dirty green sea appeared underneath the planes and the infinite blue sky under their heads. The service patrol lasted 24 hours, and after that they had 48 hours break.

There Hájek recognized the new face of a before unknown France, one with whom he did not agree, and only bitterness remained in him after seeing how the French treated affairs.

The pilots could use their leisure time to visit the cities on the coast, but there was a rule that they could not leave camp alone, that always two soldiers must travel together. They soon found out why. The soldiers always took the train; it was full of indigenous Arabs, and these two soldiers were always sitting alone in the compartment. People overcrowded the wagon's corridor. Everyone who passed their coupe looked at them with wrath, but no one took a seat beside them. The pilots did not understand and waved to people encouraging them to take a seat. After a long time they finally found an interpreter with whom they were able to speak French, and after his instruction some people took seats. The Arabs were surprised, that people other than French can be in the uniforms of their rulers. It was for the Arabs very difficult to pronounce the word 'Czechoslovakia.' Hájek and his companion had to give them a speech about where they came from and that they were here to fight against Hitler. Speaking with indigenous Arabs they found how churlish the French are to Arabs, that the French demeanor to them was like occupier and occupied, and that the Arabs despised the French to death.

On another such free time break they went to an Arab village. Through the village ran a large river. In the middle of the river was a marvelous, enchanting small island verdant with tropical flora. They decided immediately to get out to this island.

A small boat was docked at the shore opposite the island. They were thinking to take this boat and float themselves to the island. As the Arabs saw what the soldiers wanted to do, they started screaming and were zealously gesticulating. The soldiers did not understand what was happening. After a while, one of the pilots said to Hájek, "Leave them alone, and let us go to the island." They floated away on the boat toward the island, and large clusters of people were watching them from ashore. When the soldiers were not so far from the shore, suddenly a big snake smashed against them with a terrible hissing noise. It was the great python, 6 meters long, 50 centimeters in diameter. They quickly turned the boat around and raced back to the shore, happily landing on dry ground and finally understanding the previous interest of the Arabs.

The rest of the story also needs to be clarified. The Arabian clans were engaged in permanent hostility with their French occupiers, and there were still fights between the French colonial army and their residents. That is why the camp was surrounded by a barbed wire barrier and under permanent guard, at night particularly. For hygienic reasons the latrine had been located approximately 100 meters outside of the camp. Everyone who needed to go to the latrine had to pass by the guard. The guard service was very taut and responsible. Just imagine yourself, the terrible heat all day and you are exhausted from this, and sleep is pertinacious while an enemy comes slinking and silently killing by knife.

Once Václav was telling us this story. It was something like three months they were in the camp, and they had become accustomed to this lonely spot, when at an officer lunch, their commandant, who was in a very good mood, told them the following story.

> "Dear fellows, now I can tell you something about a tragedy of our predecessors. One soldier had dysentery, went to the latrine, and was there for a long time. When he was going back to camp it was for him conspicuous that there was no guard on the gate. He reached his barrack and now he found that his fellows had been decapitated, heads entirely separated from bodies, only blood around everywhere. In panic, he ran to the commandant's tent, and there was the

same scene. The entire garrison to the last man had been slaughtered. In dread, afraid that he could be killed, he ran to the kitchen, in a hurry he packed some food and took something to drink, and he ran out of the camp to the closest military camp, a distance of something like 150 km. He was running for three nights when he fortunately and finally reached this military camp. He reported the terrible destiny of his fellows. The clearance platoon found that nothing had been stolen or destroyed. The Arabs most probably came slinking and silently slaughtered all the men then left without leaving any marks." We were all shivering while he told us this story. We swore to ourselves silently, that knowing what happened to our predecessors, nobody would be as able to take us in that manner here.

The war had dramatic changes in 1940. France had been beaten in Europe, the French army outside of France was dispersed, and not all of the French soldiers were ready to listen to old Marshal Petain in the occupied part of France. The Czech pilots were thinking to escape to the neighboring English dominion, Iraq. One of them who knew English secretly crossed the border, and on the English boundary guardroom he arranged for their escape: At a specified time they were hidden near the guardroom. Suddenly and under very dramatic circumstances came a British army lorry very close to the Syrian border. The driver pretended to be drunk. He stopped for a while and our soldiers climbed into the lorry and the lorry–in front of the surprised Syrian guards on the camels–drove off without any shot being fired.

They were welcomed with open arms into the British service. Great Britain was ready to defend itself after the defeat of France, Belgium, and the Netherlands, but there was a lack of pilots in the Royal Air Force. The British put the Czech pilots on a ship, and due to the Mediterranean Sea being full of mines and German U-boats, the ship floated through the Suez Canal and around the entire African continent until they opportunely landed in some harbor in England. The journey lasted 45 days and was very dramatic. The ship went through storms and nearly wrecked. Seasickness was the sole story.

And England? It would be a whole book of exciting impressions, because war seemed infinite. Václav gladly and dutifully participated in the Battle of Britain and as the commandant of the 313 Squadron. Hájek's story is described in the book Wings in Fire written by H.J. Slipka, Orbis Prague 1945. Most details about participation of the Czech pilots in WWII you can find in the books like In Flight from Beginning to the End written by

Jarnslav Bala, Orbis Prague 1945 or in <u>On the West Front</u> from 1964 or time to time in some illustrated magazines.

Václav returned back to his motherland in summer 1945, with a lot of decorations on his chest. I think he came home also with a variety of demons, because from among 14 of his pilot-fellows, with whom he went through all, there returned only three. He always had tears in his eyes, always, when he was remembering them.

What can we say about that all? Can we call that good luck in life? Or coincidence? It will always be the inexplicable question that he who so often was so close to death got off from all of that to live.

Uncommon man: He returned as a modest soldier, never speaking about himself, only when someone asked him. No one was surprised, when after his return to the motherland he was commended — for his merits and experiences in military aviation — to the Department of Air Forces of the Czech Ministry of Defense. He accompanied the leading general by plane on the inspection of different garrisons all around Czechoslovakia. Then he got married. He told us that coming from his personal war experience, he had had several fights and arguments with the leading bureaucratic generals of the older generation regarding the new conception of Czech Air Forces. He was shifted to

Brno in 1948 as an instructor of some military academy. But after a couple of months he was fired from this military academy and later from the Air Forces as well. He found a job again in the same factory where he started.

Hájek's family spent all their free time mostly in Ohnišov. Václav liked that place because there he could be involved in his hobby, hunting. We were surprised that he was not too lazy to get up very early each morning and to go with the other hunters to wait for deer. He was really a jack-of-all-trades. He was able to repair everything; he always gave good advice. Generously, he offered his own time to grandmother to repair the rabbit hutch. He helped with the harvest on the fields. When they came to Ohnišov it was like a holiday for all of us. We were silent when he told us his stories from the world, from countries for us unknown.

The years 1947 and 1948 passed in such a manner. We were expecting him in summer 1949, but he excused himself because he had to go to some holiday job for two weeks. He indicated that they would come home after the job was over. But they did not come. They cleared off together with their 18-month-old daughter. Not until November 1949 did we obtain a message from them that they were back in England, back in England where he had spent almost five years of his life. He had a very high opinion of the Britons. But this is a completely new chapter, not finished yet.

I have written down this story to remember them and in memory of the 20-year anniversary of the day I first met this good man, who has a lot of merit for human society and who shall also be the pattern for all his progeny.

My only wish is that should he return back at once, that he would review these memories and complete them so as to keep them for the future generations.

~Václav Mach

# Police Blotter

*(10* June 1999) ROLLOVER — Two cars collided, one of which subsequently rolled over, on Mansfield Avenue near Buttonwood Lane on Saturday, leaving one person injured. Police said Erin Sprinkle, 23, of Massachusetts, was driving a 1993 Saturn southbound on Mansfield Avenue about 5 p.m. when she attempted to turn onto Buttonwood Lane, turning into the path of a northbound 1997 BMW driven by 51-year-old Olga Haack of Knollwood Lane in Darien. The vehicles collided with such force that Haack's BMW rolled onto its roof. Explorer Post 53 personnel treated Haack at the scene and then transported her to Stamford Hospital, where she was treated and released. Sprinkle was ticketed for failing to grant right of way.[20]

---

[20] The Darien Times, Thursday, 10 June 1999.

# Rest In Peace

$\mathscr{V}$áclav Hájek died Monday, 14 June 1999 at Wilton Meadows Health Care Center in Wilton, Connecticut. He was 86. Born 30 January 1913, in Prague, Czechoslovakia, he came to the United States as a refugee.[21] A 1935 graduate of the University of Prague, he joined the British Royal Air Force at the outset of World War II. He flew Spitfires throughout the war as a squadron leader for the 313th squadron of Czech pilots. He was an engineer at Lockheed in Burbank, California, and later in Los Angeles, retiring in 1987. His daughter, Olga Hájek Haack as well as two granddaughters, Anne Květa Haack and Catharine Marie Haack, survive him. His wife, Květa Mach Hájek, predeceased him. A private burial will be held in the Holy Cross Cemetery in Inglewood, California. Memorial contributions may be made to Young Life Darien.

~~~

Westlake Village, June 1999

With loving thoughts to Olga, Tom, Anne, and Kati:

---

[21] Technically on INS paperwork, he came over as a citizen, subject, or national of Great Britain.

The words in this card are so true.

**May your hearts find comfort in knowing that your loved one waits for you in that beautiful place where there will be no more tears or parting.**

All of us who knew the rare, beautiful qualities of a true gentleman won't ever forget him. God be with you. Please donate the money to General Hájek's favorite charity.

Love,
Irma and Joe Séda

# One Fine Day

When through sweet sleep Václav finally entered into life everafter, he had been living at Wilton Meadows for almost a decade. "That drive. Every single day for over nine years I went to see him," remembers Mom of the 25-minute drive from our home. We would bring him cookies or little mini cans of Budweiser to hearken of his Czech home and make his assisted living more fun.

The day he died, I was living in Boston and working in Wellesley. Mom's rollover was a few days prior, and she had called Wilton Meadows relaying that due to an accident she could not come for her daily visits. We wonder in hindsight if Grandpa Hájek thought the visitation cessation was permanent and thus exhaled accordingly to close the curtain on this life.

Our immediate family met in Los Angeles along with a few friends Grandpa Hájek had made in Southern California. Květa had been buried there decades earlier, and his wish was to be beside her. He was laid to rest in uniform. The humble dignity of it all most overwhelmed me.

I cannot recall if we sang Amazing Grace though it comes to heart that we did. Timelessness came poignantly to the present for all Eternity. When we've been there ten thousand years, bright shining as the sun, we've no less days to sing God's praise than when we first begun. "Our whole business in this life is to restore to health the eye of the heart whereby God may be seen," writes Saint Augustine. God outside of time created time and entered time to redeem creation to Eternity. Were the world a perfect art, we would each take our part in that redemption. Grandpa Hájek certainly did.

After the wake, we buried him in what I recall as a beautiful field, a cemetery where the tombstones were horizontally laid in the earth as opposed to vertically sticking up all over the place. The sun shined clear yellow light, the sky stretched bright blue, and the grass grew a brilliant green. There might or might not have been flowers we buried with the casket when it lowered into the earth. What I recall is how a paradoxical feeling of lightness came over us, for Václav was finally reunited with his Květa in the ever after.

It is curious to note that whereas Květa entered eternity 15 June 1960, Václav flew his final flight from earth to eternity one day ahead, 39 years later, 14 June 1999. If time truly folds in on itself, perhaps he was there to welcome her arrival. Perhaps Puccini sang somewhere as he soared, "Dear Baby wife of mine, dear Blossom, I have returned."

# Dedication

This book is dedicated to all those who have
come before us.
This book is dedicated to my Daughter. I knew that
as God put the stars in the sky He could bring you
to me for this sweet set of moments that are our
days together.
Remember your destiny.

S.D.G.